THE RIVER OF LOVE

When they had gone back to the yacht, the Duke took her down to his private cabin to put his arms round her.

"You are mine," he said. "Whatever happened in the past, we are now together, and I swear that as long as we shall live, I will never lose you."

Then he was kissing her until Irisa felt that they had found a special Heaven in which there was nobody else, not even the gods but only themselves.

Bantam Books by Barbara Cartland
Ask your bookseller for the books you have missed

Barbara Cartland's Library of Love Series
   THE OBSTACLE RACE

About Barbara Cartland
   CRUSADER IN PINK

The River
of
Love

Barbara Cartland

BANTAM BOOKS
TORONTO • NEW YORK • LONDON • SYDNEY

THE RIVER OF LOVE

A Bantam Book/October 1981

ISBN 0-553-20013-5

Published simultaneously in the United States and Canada

Bantam Books are published by Bantam Books, Inc. Its trade-
mark, consisting of the words ''Bantam Books'' and the por-
trayal of a rooster, is Registered in U.S. Patent and Trademark
Office and in other countries. Marca Registrada. Bantam
Books, Inc., 666 Fifth Avenue, New York, New York 10103

Author's Note

Many Greeks visited ancient Egypt, but it was the Romans who began collecting Egyptian antiquities, and Sphinxes and statues of the Pharaohs adorned the Palaces of the Roman Emperors.

Demand for antiques from Europe in the early 1830s encouraged tomb-robbing. In this way, the great collections of the British Museum, the Louvre, Berlin, etc., were built up. The Valley of the Kings, however, aroused only a lukewarm interest until in 1922, when Howard Carter, financed by Lord Carnaervon, discovered the tomb of Tutankhamen.

On my first visit to Luxor in the '20s, I met Howard Carter at the Tomb and saw the dazzling display of treasures it contained.

The magic I felt then in Luxor was intensified on my second visit, over thirty years later, into a spiritual awareness which I have tried to portray in this novel.

Chapter One

1892

"I have something to tell you."

The Duke of Darleston, who was just thinking sleepily that he should return to his own bedroom, roused himself to ask:

"What is it?"

"Edward Thetford has asked me to—marry him!"

There was silence before the Duke said:

"I think you would be wise to accept him, Myrtle. He is slightly pompous but rich and good-natured."

There was no response for a moment. Then Lady Garforth said hesitantly:

"I suppose—you would not—marry me?"

The Duke smiled.

"I cannot remember if it was Oscar Wilde or Lillie Langtry who said that a good lover makes a bad husband."

"It was the Prince of Wales!" Lady Garforth replied. "And it is certainly true where he is concerned."

"As it would be for me."

"We have been so happy," Myrtle Garforth said with a little sob in her voice, "and I love you, Dasher, as you well know."

"Thetford will make you a good husband. Does he know about us?"

"I am quite sure he suspects, but it is not something he would put into words, and he certainly would not embarrass me by asking questions!"

The Duke laughed.

"If I know Thetford, he will know only what he wants to know and will ignore the rest. Marry him, Myrtle. You will be able to twist him round your little finger, and the Thetford diamonds, which I believe are very fine, will become you."

There was silence again.

Then Lady Garforth exclaimed tearfully: "Oh, Dasher!" and turned to hide her face against his shoulder.

The Duke held her close and thought as he did so that she was a very sweet person and he was very fond of her.

They had enjoyed a fiery but at the same time an amicable relationship for the last five months. Inevitably, however, he had found himself thinking that Myrtle's love tied him to her, and if there was one thing of which he was afraid, it was of being tied.

The Duke's nickname of "Dasher" was an extremely apt one, and he had earned it from the moment he was born.

His father, the fourth Duke, had just watched his horse *The Dasher* pass the winning-post on the Epsom Race-Course a length in front of the rest of the field, when his Comptroller, pushing his way through the crowds outside the Jockey Club, came to his side.

For a moment it was difficult to speak to his Master because his friends were congratulating him on his win.

"Well done!"

"A tremendous victory!"

"The Blue Riband of the Turf, and nobody deserves it more!"

The Duke was just about to move away to see his jockey weigh in, when he found his Comptroller at his elbow.

"Excuse me, Your Grace."

"What is it, Hunter?" the Duke asked testily.

"Her Grace has just been delivered of a son!"

"A son?" The Duke roared out the word and his voice arrested the attention of quite a number of men near him.

"A son! At last!" he ejaculated.

His closest friends echoed the cry, well aware that after four daughters, a son was what the Duke wanted more than anything else in the world.

Then he laughed and it shook his large frame.

"A son, and three weeks early!" he cried. "It seems to me he intends to be a bit of a Dasher too!"

From that moment, the Marquis of Darle was never known by any other name.

He was duly christened after his grandfather, his God-parents, and his mother's favourite brother, but he became The Dasher by name and inevitably The Dasher by nature.

Extremely good-looking, by the time he left Eton it seemed as if few women could resist his engaging smile and what was undoubtedly a raffish face.

It was easy to understand why he was so irresistible.

It was not only his good looks, his social position, and the immense wealth of the Darleston family. It was because he found life an exciting, amusing adventure.

"What the hell have you got to be so happy about?"

his friends would sometimes ask, when he seemed to radiate a joy of living which they somehow missed.

But it meant that nothing lasted permanently where The Dasher was concerned, least of all women.

As he grew older, they came into his life in such numbers that even the most inveterate gossips lost count.

The strange thing, unusual in most men's *affaires de coeur,* was that the women he loved so fleetingly were seldom bitter or even resentful when he parted from them.

Undoubtedly many of them had aching hearts, but in some extraordinary and quite unusual way they thought of The Dasher with gratitude for the happiness he had given them and were prepared to defend him against his enemies.

It was inevitable that quite a number of people, especially men, were jealous and envied him, but he also had many friends who were concerned with him as a person and with his sporting rather than his amatory activities.

There was little in the Sporting World which The Dasher had not attempted. He raced his own horses, riding even in the Grand National, and had made his name in the Polo-Field.

He had sailed his own yacht in the races at Cowes, and had nearly been drowned trying to beat the record when paddling a light canoe.

As a fast bowler he had captained the First Eleven at Eton, owned the champion greyhound for two years, and naturally was Master of his own foxhounds.

The shooting on his Estates had been greatly improved since he had inherited the title, and the Prince of Wales had said only the previous year that he would rather shoot at Darle Castle than anywhere else.

All these interests, numerous though they were,

seemed to leave The Dasher time to want more and yet more out of life.

"It is almost," somebody had once said, "as if he is racing against time, or perhaps seeking something that he is afraid he may miss if he does not hurry."

It was as if this idea came to Myrtle Garforth's mind now, as she asked:

"What are you looking for in a wife, Dasher?"

"I have no intention of getting married," the Duke replied.

"But you will have to sooner or later. Do not forget, your father had four daughters before you arrived."

"My relatives leave me no choice of forgetting that!"

He was thinking, and he was very honest with himself, that it was not surprising that he had been spoilt as a child.

His four sisters had adored him, and as far as his father was concerned the sun and the moon rose for him alone.

He remembered his mother, when he was very small, saying:

"You must not spoil him. If you give him his own way in everything, he will be impossible by the time he grows up."

What had saved the Duke from becoming impossible was the fact that he was extremely intelligent.

He was well aware of his good fortune in being born into a family which was respected and admired by everyone from the Monarch downwards. Even the Queen, extremely critical of the nobility, especially those who surrounded her son, had no fault to find with the fourth Duke and his wife.

And although some of the present Duke's more outrageous exploits must have been repeated to her, she treated him with an indulgence that she seldom granted to any other young man of his age.

The Duke's critics said sourly that Her Majesty had always been susceptible to flattery.

But actually the Duke did not flatter the Queen. He merely talked to her, as he talked to every women, as if he found her both attractive and interesting.

And like all women the Queen responded to it like a flower opening its petals to the sun.

In fact, the only problem in his life, if you could call it that, was how to avoid being married to one of the innumerable females who were determined by hook or by crook to shackle him for life either to themselves or to their daughters.

"One day, Dasher," Myrtle Garforth said now, "you will fall in love."

For once she actually surprised the Duke.

"Are you suggesting," he enquired, "that I have never been?"

"I am not suggesting it. I am stating a fact!"

The Duke was about to laugh at her for saying something so absurd, when it suddenly struck him that it might be the truth.

He had always thought himself to be in love when he was attracted by some beautiful face turned towards his and saw two eyes looking at him with an unmistakable invitation in their depths.

Whenever he felt a response within himself and knew an irrepressible desire to kiss a pair of provocative lips, he would tell himself that Cupid had struck again and he was in love!

Now, looking back at what had invariably been a short-lived rapture, an ecstasy which had slowly but inevitably subsided, he wondered if Myrtle was right.

She was aware that she had made him think, and, settling herself a little more comfortably, she said:

"I love you, Dasher, and I know I shall love you all

my life, and there will never be another man to compare with you. But I am not so foolish as to think that what you feel for me is something which will last."

"How do you know that?" the Duke enquired.

"Because, darling, you have never been in love in the way that has inspired men and women since the beginning of time so that if necessary they would be prepared to die for it."

"I understand what you are trying to say," the Duke remarked, "but do you really think that that sort of love—the love of the poets, the musicians, the romantics—is likely to happen to a man like me? I am a roamer."

"Of course you are," Myrtle agreed. "But that is because you have not found what you seek."

"I am certainly not seeking love, if that is what you mean," the Duke answered sharply. "I am quite prepared to admit that what you are talking about exists, but I am very content with what I find and—enjoy."

His arm tightened round Myrtle's soft body as he said the last word, and she responded by putting her arm round his neck as if to pull his head down to hers. Then she changed her mind.

"Because I love you, Dasher," she said, "I would like you to find real happiness. And I have the feeling, although I may be wrong, that one day you will find it."

"When I do, I will let you know!" the Duke said lightly.

"No, I am serious. You give so much happiness to others, in all sorts of different ways, that I want you to find the greatest happiness which human beings can attain, and that is—real love."

"You are trying to make me dissatisfied," the Duke complained, "and I understand you think I am missing something! In which case, you know as well as I do that I shall do everything in my power to find it—and win it!"

"I hope what you are saying is true," Myrtle said, "but perhaps it would only be fair if you failed. You have too much already."

"Now I am quite certain that you are trying to punish me for saying you should marry Thetford!" the Duke exclaimed.

"That is unkind," Myrtle protested. "I only want you to have the best out of life."

"That is what I thought I had already."

There was silence as the Duke thought over what she had said.

In a way it annoyed him to think she might be right.

He had always been so sure that everything he wanted was within his reach, and while he enjoyed having to strive for what he wanted, deep down he always had the conviction that sooner or later he would be the victor.

Even now it was impossible for him to believe that there was some strange sort of love which so far had evaded him.

He thought of the women with whom he had been infatuated, if that was the right word, and the pleasure they had given him and he had given them.

The excitement they had engendered together had sometimes been like fireworks sparkling against the darkness of the sky, at others like flowers growing at the water's edge and the lap of waves on golden sand.

Love, many diverse and different types of love, but always the initial fiery flames dying down to a mere glow.

"Why should I want anything different?" the Duke asked defiantly.

"I have made you think," a soft voice broke in on his thoughts, "and that is an achievement in itself."

"You are making me feel as if I were abnormal," the Duke said crossly.

"Not abnormal," Myrtle protested, "but different! A

King, a Chieftain, a Pharaoh, and very different from any ordinary man I have ever known."

There was a little pause. Then the Duke said:

"Is that really the truth?"

"Of course it is," Myrtle replied. "You must be aware, Dasher, that there is nobody like you. That is what makes you so exciting. You make one feel almost as if you do not belong in these modern times but have stepped out of history or perhaps a different planet."

She gave a little laugh before she went on:

"Perhaps you have been—what is the word for having lived before and being reborn?"

"Reincarnated."

"Yes, that is it," Myrtle agreed. "Perhaps you have been reincarnated after being, as I said just now, a King in some Eastern country, or a Pharaoh in Egypt."

"Or a slave, a monkey, or a reptile!" the Duke said teasingly.

"No, that would be impossible!" Myrtle cried. "Your talents, or whatever they are, are far too developed."

In his determination not to be serious, the Duke said:

"And all this because I suggested you should accept Edward Thetford's proposal of marriage!"

"And you—refused to marry—me!"

"I want you to continue to love me," the Duke said, "and that is certainly something you would not do if I were your husband."

"It would almost be worth the—unhappiness of being—jealous like—Princess Alexandra, rather than— lose you—altogether."

The Duke did not answer, and after a moment she said:

"Very well, I shall marry Edward. But please, Dasher, let us forget him for just a little while longer."

The Duke could not resist the pleading in her voice. He turned round, pulled her nearer to him, and his lips were on hers.

But even as he kissed her, he was asking himself:

"Where is the love that I am missing?"

* * *

Harry Settingham was fast asleep when he became aware that somebody was pulling back the curtains over the windows, and thought before he opened his eyes that he was very tired.

He had certainly gone to bed late, and perhaps he had drunk too much of Dasher's excellent wine, for he certainly had no wish at the moment to face another day.

He suddenly realised that it was not his valet who had opened the curtains to let in the daylight, but somebody very much larger, who now advanced to sit down on the end of his bed.

"Dasher!" he exclaimed. "What do you want so early?"

"I want to talk to you, Harry."

With an effort, Harry opened his eyes wider.

"What about? What time is it?"

"About six o'clock, I think."

"Six o'clock? Good Heavens, Dasher, what has happened?"

"I have decided to go exploring and I want you to come with me!"

"Exploring?"

With an effort, Harry Settingham moved himself higher against his pillows before he asked:

"What has upset you?"

"Nothing has upset me," the Duke replied. "I have merely decided that I want to get away from all the things we have been doing week after week, month after month, with monotonous regularity."

"I think you are mad!" Harry Settingham exclaimed. "Anything less monotonous than your life I cannot imagine! You were hunting in Leicestershire last week, and we were supposed to be hunting tomorrow, if the ground is not too hard, and yet you talk of going away!"

"I am leaving for Egypt immediately!"

"Egypt!" Harry cried. "What on earth for?"

"I think it will be interesting, and I want to see the land of the Pharaohs."

"I am not sure I wish to look at a lot of old ruins," Harry said. "Bertie went there last year and said it was a 'dead and alive' place, except that there were some pretty dancers in Cairo."

"I am not going for that sort of thing," the Duke said. "I am serious, Harry. I want to look into the past of Egypt, and see other parts of the world."

"Are you bored with Myrtle?" Harry asked, as if the idea had suddenly come to him.

"I am very fond of Myrtle," the Duke said firmly, "but Thetford has asked her to marry him and I have advised her to accept."

"So he has come up to scratch, has he?" Harry remarked. "The betting at White's since you took over was that he would cool off."

"You can always be quite certain that any conclusion reached by members of White's, who have nothing else to do, is invariably wrong!"

Harry laughed.

"What you are really saying is that you dislike their talking about your private affairs. Good Heavens, Dasher, you must be aware that you bring light and laughter into their otherwise rather dull lives."

The Duke laughed too, as if he could not help it.

"I suppose in that case I must be willing to oblige," he remarked. "But you have not yet accepted my invitation."

"To come to Egypt with you? Of course, if you want me. Who else are you thinking of taking?"

"I am not quite certain," the Duke said. "It is something I want to discuss with you."

"At this hour of the morning?"

"As I wish to leave as soon as possible, the invitations will have to be sent out immediately."

Harry put back his head against the pillows and laughed.

"That, Dasher, is exactly like you! Most people, if they are going abroad for any length of time, especially to places they have never visited before, spend months preparing for it. All right, you win! And I will not protest about losing my 'beauty sleep.'"

"You can make up for it on the voyage," the Duke said unfeelingly. "Now, who will be amusing for what may be quite a considerable length of time?"

There was an hour's discussion before finally they chose four people.

Harry Settingham had been the Duke's closest friend all through his life. They had been at Eton together, had gone up to Oxford together, and both had served for three years in the Household Brigade until the Duke had inherited the title.

Although he had enjoyed the comradeship in his Regiment, he had longed for the activity of war, which had not come their way, owing to the fact that the Houshold Brigade was so seldom sent abroad.

Camps and manoeuvres were not the same thing, and Harry had been aware that The Dasher was already champing at the bit when, on his father's death, he could resign with dignity and without reproach.

Because the two men were such close friends, it had been assumed that Harry Settingham would follow the Duke's example.

It was also generally accepted that Harry had a

restraining influence on The Dasher, but only he knew that actually nobody had any influence on a man who was unique, especially when it came to intellect.

If Myrtle Garforth thought the Duke had never been in love, Harry was sure of it.

He told himself it was unlikely that the Duke would ever find any woman to satisfy him while there were so many who could offer him the physical attractions of Venus but who could not hold his mind as well as his body.

Now as he listened to the Duke planning their trip to Egypt, he told himself that he might have expected it, since he had been aware that The Dasher's interest in Myrtle Garforth was inevitably waning.

He had always liked Myrtle and thought her one of the nicest and most understanding of the many lovely women with whom the Duke had been enamoured.

She was kind to other women, pleasant to the Duke's friends, and he had never heard her say anything spiteful or unkind about anybody.

At the same time, while she had an average intelligence, she was not well read.

Very few women were, when inevitably their education had been entrusted to one badly paid Governess who had been expected to teach every subject in the curriculum.

This was the ordinary, accepted pattern in any aristocratic household, where every penny was expended on the sons and as little as possible on the daughters.

Kept in the School-Room, out of touch with ordinary everyday life until the moment they made their début, the girls were then supposed to blossom like flowers and make a distinguished Social marriage within the first two years of their "coming out."

This was, of course, arranged by their mothers with little or no regard for their daughters' feelings in the matter.

Only when they had the ring on their finger and were able to enjoy the company of other young married women did they develop the sophistication and poise expected of them.

The extraordinary thing, Harry had often thought, was that they did in fact become elegant and witty, with a polish and a sophistication that made them outstanding even in other countries.

The ladies who centred round the Prince of Wales were obvious examples of those qualities, and although The Dasher and Harry were almost a generation younger, they expected the same standard from their contemporaries.

'It is a pity about Myrtle,' Harry thought now, 'but doubtless her place will soon be filled.'

Aloud he asked:

"Are you really intending to include Lady Cairns in your party?"

When the Duke had first mentioned her name, Harry had hesitated because he thought that although she was extremely beautiful, she might not have the same kind nature as Myrtle.

Lily Cairns had obviously aroused the Duke's interest the previous week when he had been introduced to her at Marlborough House.

Because she had been living in the North, she was new to London, but there was nothing countrified about her appearance.

With her auburn hair, her white skin, and a slightly enigmatic look in her eyes, she had caught everybody's attention when she had appeared, including that of the Prince.

"This is your first visit to Marlborough House?" Harry had heard His Royal Highness ask in his deep, rather guttural voice. "I understand you have only just arrived in London."

"I have been living in Scotland, Sire."

"And has the 'Land of the Haggis' so much to offer that it has made you neglect us here in the South?" the Prince enquired.

The smile that Lily had given the elderly Prince was very enticing.

"I have merely returned home, Sire, now that I am a widow."

Later in the evening Harry had seen the Duke gravitating irresistibly towards the corner of the room where Lady Cairns was undoubtedly "holding court."

Although he had not realised it at the time, he knew now that it had been the moment when Myrtle's fate was sealed, for The Dasher was once again drawn to a new and lovely face.

In answer to Harry's question, the Duke said now quite seriously:

"Lily Cairns has lived in Scotland for so long that she should be used to a certain amount of hardship, not that I expect there will be much aboard *The Mermaid*."

"I hope not," Harry said. "If I am to be uncomfortable, I have no intention of going with you."

"After that extremely selfish remark," the Duke said, "I shall take you riding in the middle of the desert on a camel. You are getting soft, Harry, and it would doubtless do you good to climb to the top of one of the pyramids."

"I refuse to talk about this absurd trip any longer," Harry complained. "I want to go back to sleep. Arrange anything you like—bring anyone with us who will amuse you, not me, so that you will not be bored stiff within twenty-four hours, and I am prepared, O Master, to obey thy command!"

The Duke laughed.

"All right, Harry, go to sleep. I will have everything arranged, including an alluring houri to keep you amused."

"You can pick one up in Cairo," Harry replied. "Remember, Dasher, most women do not look their best when they are being seasick!"

The Duke laughed again, walked to the window to flick back the curtains, and left the room.

Harry shut his eyes, but, not unnaturally, he did not fall asleep immediately.

Instead, he was thinking that it was very like the Duke suddenly to move to pastures new.

It was in fact one of the things that made him so interesting, when like a small boy he would play truant on all his responsibilities and embark on some new adventure without the slightest hesitation or any anticipation of whether it would be a success or a failure.

It was what made life with him so interesting, Harry thought. Then he came to the conclusion that it was surprising that it had not happened earlier.

It was now nearly a year since the Duke had rushed off at a moment's notice to do something entirely different from what anybody might have expected of him.

The reason for his being almost static was that before Myrtle he had had an extremely passionate love-affair, which had lasted for seven or eight months, with the wife of a famous Politician.

The reason that it had lasted so long was that they could not be together as much as they wished.

Although the lady's husband was conveniently kept busy at the House of Commons, she also had to spend quite a considerable amount of time with him in his Constituency and accompanying him on occasional trips abroad.

Surprisingly, because it was unusual, The Dasher's heart seemed to grow fonder in her absence, and he was awaiting her eagerly on her return.

She was certainly, Harry had thought at the time, well worth waiting for.

Her beauty at twenty-seven was at its height, and she was half-Russian, which gave her a mysterious allure that seemed to hold the Duke as if it were a magnet.

And yet, even with her the affair, as happened with all his other loves, had ground to a halt, and although nobody was surprised, Harry had anticipated the inevitable.

The Dasher had found that there was nothing more to know or to discover about the lady in question, and therefore he was no longer interested.

It was Harry who was aware that the Duke really took from the women who loved him all they had to give, then when his curiosity was assuaged he needed fresh stimulus from someone else.

Although he had the greatest admiration and deepest affection for his friend, he sometimes wondered if the Duke was too richly endowed by nature.

It was not fair for one man to have so much and to expect to find the counterpart of himself in a female body.

But there was certainly no point in worrying about a man who seemed so happy and who enjoyed life with an exuberance which everybody with whom he came in contact found infectious.

When the Duke entered a room, the tempo seemed to quicken. Women became brighter and more animated, men wittier and more amusing.

Harry often thought that the most ordinary, boring party could be transformed when the Duke was a guest.

It was one of the reasons why every hostess prayed that he would accept her invitation and was genuinely elated by the sight of him when he appeared.

"Egypt!" Harry exclaimed to himself. "Now, why on earth would The Dasher want to go there, of all places?"

He felt personally that ruins were invariably depressing, and the Mummies of those who had been dead for centuries were not the sort of women the Duke would find interesting.

Still, it was something new!

He had never been to Egypt, nor had the Duke, and the idea of steaming up the Nile in *The Mermaid* would certainly be different from chasing a fox or watching The Dasher's superb horses moving far too easily in the Spring Steeple-Chases.

"Anyway, he will have Lily!" Harry said to himself.

He closed his eyes and fell asleep.

Chapter Two

Lily Cairns stepped out of the old-fashioned carriage in which she had been driving in the Park, and, carrying her muff which was of sable, walked slowly up the steps and into the Hall of the house in Belgrave Square.

The Butler, grey-haired and slightly bent with age, said in the loud voice of someone who is deaf:

"The Duke of Darleston has called to see you, M'Lady!"

Lily stood still for a moment. Then with a composure which she was far from feeling she asked:

"Is His Grace in the Drawing-Room?"

"Yes, M'Lady."

Lily hesitated, then with a swiftness which was echoed by the beat of her heart she ran upstairs to her bedroom, pulling off her long fur-trimmed coat before she reached the door.

She flung both her coat and her muff down on the

19

bed and moved quickly to the dressing-table to remove
her very attractive bonnet.

As she did so, she looked at her reflection in the
mirror, and her eyes, which had been wide with excitement, narrowed a little as she concentrated.

This was what she had expected. This was what she
had prayed for!

Now the Duke was waiting for her downstairs, and
she had taken the first step towards her goal.

Lily Cairns was shrewd, calculating, and insatiably
ambitious. She had determined since the age of fifteen
not to be crushed by poverty or to live a nondescript life
as a nobody in the wilds of Perthshire.

Her father, Roland Standish, who was a gentleman
but an impoverished one, had, because he was keen on
sport, accepted the position of Agent on the large Estate
of Sir Ewan Cairns when Lily was twelve years old.

Before that they had lived in the South, but her
father had disliked being too poor to afford horses for
riding and hunting, and he found it more and more difficult to patronise the best Clubs or even to pay the rent
for his lodgings in London.

Lily's mother had fortunately died when she was
very young.

Being a sharp-witted child, Lily had soon learnt that
there was some mystery about her mother, and her father's relatives spoke of her with pursed lips.

Other people insinuated, although they did not actually say so, that it was lucky for Lily and her father that
she was no longer with them.

When Lily questioned her aunts, all they said was
that her mother had "gone to God."

But it was obvious from the tone of their voices and
the expression in their eyes that they thought she was far
more likely to be in a very different place.

It was only when she was much older that Lily learnt

that her mother had been the daughter of a Wine Merchant to whom her father had owed money.

She had been exceedingly attractive, and when the Wine Merchant learnt that his daughter had been seduced by one of his largest debtors, it was not surprising that he had brought pressure to bear on him to make her an honest woman.

He also offered to write off or cancel a debt which had been outstanding for far too long.

Unfortunately, the money the Wine Merchant contributed towards the marriage came to an end with his daughter's death.

It was then that Roland Standish found the suggestion that he should go and stay with Sir Ewan Cairns in Scotland as an excuse for foisting his daughter on one of his relatives, while he tried a different life from the one he had been leading up until then.

He was in fact by nature a sportsman, and although as a game-shot he was at first, through lack of practice, not very proficient, he soon improved.

At the same time, he appreciated the large, comfortable grey-stone house on the edge of the moors and the companionship of his host.

They shot over the Estate, caught salmon in the river, and entertained the local Lairds and their wives, who were prepared to travel long distances in any sort of weather in order to enjoy congenial company.

It was only when Roland Standish suggested that he should return South that Sir Ewan offered him a house on the Estate and a salary which he felt he would be stupid to refuse.

It meant giving up the friends he had known in London, but that loss was offset by the fact that he still had a number of outstanding debts there which might be forgotten if he stayed long enough in the North.

Finally having agreed, he sent for Lily, and on her

arrival was pleased to find that she had not only grown
taller in her absence but had become exceedingly attractive.

To Lily, who had hated the restrictive life she had
lived with her father's cousin, who seemed intent on
finding fault with everything she did or thought, life in
Scotland meant a new freedom and to begin with was
sheer delight.

Then as the years passed she began to understand
how everything depended on the whim and goodwill of
her father's employer.

At over fifty, Sir Ewan was, thanks to the life he led,
still a healthy, active man, and he was also an autocrat,
very conscious of his ancient Scottish lineage.

Like the ancient Chieftains, he expected not only
obedience but an adoration which was not so readily
given as it had been in the past.

But no longer, although the change was slow in coming to the Highlands, were the servants prepared to be
as subservient as they had been over the years.

Lily soon realised that Sir Ewan liked feeling that
her father was completely dependent on him, and that
also included herself. It became obvious that if she wanted
anything special, it was not her father who provided it
but Sir Ewan.

She was also aware that since his wife had died some
ten years earlier, he was in many ways a lonely man.

Periodic trips occurred, which Lily understood later
were to see an old friend of many years' standing who
supplied the only feminine influence in his otherwise
strictly masculine life.

By the time she was nearly seventeen she was aware
that Sir Ewan was thinking of her not as a child but as a
woman.

When her father died from pneumonia caught after
being lost on the moors in a thick fog one freezing

November night, Lily had decided to marry Sir Ewan long before he made up his mind to propose to her.

When the Funeral was over, looking sad but exceedingly beautiful in her black gown which had hastily been procured from Perth, she looked at him with misty, tearful eyes and asked in a low, childish voice she was often to use in the future:

"I know Papa has left—no money—and you will—want the house for another Agent—so perhaps I can find some sort of work in—Perth, if you will—help me."

It was then that Sir Ewan had offered her a wedding-ring and bought her a trousseau which had left her ecstatic with joy.

Never had she expected to own such lovely gowns, and she was not in the least fastidious about wearing the furs and jewellery which had been owned by the previous Lady Cairns.

They went to Edinburgh for three weeks, where Sir Ewan introduced his young bride to his shocked and disapproving relatives, but they were too much in awe of him to express their feelings openly.

Only Lily sensed what they were thinking, and it amused her.

There was Theatres to attend, besides Balls, Assemblies, and Receptions.

She also persuaded her husband to buy her more clothes and jewellery that was larger and more spectacular than any the first Lady Cairns ever owned or would have considered tasteful.

It was after three years of marriage that Lily began to think of her future.

She had known when she married that Sir Ewan had a son by his first wife, and although Alister had quarrelled with his father and lived in the South, he was heir to the Baronetcy and to the Estate.

It had not worried Lily at first, in fact she had not

even thought about Alister Cairns, whom she had never met, as having any particular impact on her own life.

But when her husband was laid up with severe influenza after getting soaked to the skin while fishing, she was suddenly aware that if he died as her father had done, she would once again be penniless.

He had been quite frank with her soon after they were married.

"I have made a new Will," he had said, speaking in a somewhat grudging manner because he always disliked discussing his private affairs with anybody, least of all a woman. "I cannot leave you much. Everything is entailed onto Alister, and I am not a rich man."

Lily had not answered for a moment, then before she could do so Sir Ewan had continued:

"You shall have everything it is possible for me to leave you, but you will have to be frugal, which is something you do not seem capable of doing at the moment."

"I am sorry if I have done—anything—wrong," Lily said in the childlike voice which never ceased to have the right effect.

"Not wrong," Sir Ewan replied, "but you are an extravagant young puss!"

The words were not a reproof but a caress. Then he said sharply in a very different voice:

"I suppose you will marry again, and you had better see that he is a rich man."

It was perhaps that more than anything else which made Lily realise that when she was a widow she would have to find a husband, and one rich enough to keep her in the manner to which she had become accustomed since her father had died.

Edinburgh had given her a taste of Society, but by now she was well aware that what she really craved was not the Scottish Capital but the English one.

She read every magazine and the social-column of every newspaper and she also listened to what the women said, which was far more informative on this score than any information she could glean from the men.

London Society had no idea how interested other parts of the country were in its doings.

Lily learnt about the mistresses of the Prince of Wales, the fascinations of the Professional Beauties, the noblemen who surrounded His Royal Highness and who vied with one another in entertaining him at their country houses and at their shoots.

It was actually somebody talking with her husband who had first mentioned the Duke of Darleston.

The bag at Darle Castle last week was over twenty-six hundred pheasants, Cairns!" he said. "I wish I had been there."

"I hear the new Duke has improved the shoot out of all recognition since he inherited," Sir Ewan replied. "But it is a long time since I shot a pheasant."

"How are your grouse this season?" his friend questioned, and the talk became exclusively Scottish.

Other people had talked about the Duke.

"I have never seen such an attractive man in my whole life!" Lily heard one pretty married woman say to another. "I saw him at several Balls when I was in London, and it does not surprise me that he is nicknamed 'The Dasher.' He is in fact the most dashing and exciting man one could dream about."

When on Lily's insistence Sir Ewan had taken her back to Edinburgh year after year, staying each time, because she pleaded with him, a little longer than the time before, she increased her knowledge of the Duke of Darleston.

The stories about him were stored away in her mind as a magpie hides its treasures in its nest.

She began to look for his name in the social-papers, the races in which his horses ran, and the Balls where his name was listed among the guests.

Even the Funerals where he occasionally represented either the Prince of Wales or occasionally the Queen did not escape her.

"If I ever go to London," Lily promised herself, "the first man I shall try to meet will be the Duke of Darleston!"

When Sir Ewan died after they had been married for nine years, she had everything planned.

She had been clever enough, when she realised that her husband was growing old and the snow and the cold winds in the winter often forced him to stay in bed, to accumulate everything she could against the future.

Although he had never mentioned it again, she had not forgotten that he had said he could leave her very little in his Will, and when it was read she found that that was undoubtedly the truth.

She had approximately five hundred pounds a year, while everything else in the Castle belonged to Alister, who appeared at his father's Funeral and instantly took over in a manner which told Lily without words that her days there were numbered.

Fortunately, she had anticipated what would happen, and she had already made plans for where she could stay in London.

She had learnt after she was married that Sir Ewan had a sister who had married one of the Senior Officers who had been stationed in Edinburgh Castle.

When General Sir Alexander Rushton retired, he and his wife had gone South to London, where Lily knew they had a house in Belgrave Square.

She had persuaded Sir Ewan, who did not particularly like his brother-in-law, to invite them to the opening of the grouse season on the twelfth of August.

The first year they had refused but the second year they had come, and Lily had exerted herself in every possible way to please and charm her sister-in-law.

There was no doubt that Lady Rushton had disapproved of her brother marrying again and a girl young enough to be his grand-daughter.

But Lily's deferential manner, her obvious and grateful adoration of her husband, and her desire to please would have melted a far harder heart than that of a woman who had no children of her own.

"You have been so kind—so wonderful to—me," Lily said, using again her childish voice when it was time for Lady Rushton to depart.

"I shall miss you," she added with what sounded curiously like a sob.

"And I shall miss you, dear," Lady Rushton said. "I will ask Ewan to bring you to stay with us in London. If that is not possible, I will try to persuade my husband to come back here another year."

"Oh, please—please do that!" Lily had begged.

She had sounded so sincere and in a way pathetic that Lady Rushton's maternal feelings had been aroused, and for years she replied regularly to Lily's effusive letters from the North.

After Sir Ewan's death, Lily had written to Lady Rushton asking if she could come and stay with her in London, and the answer was a spontaneous invitation to stay as long as she liked.

Lily had not rushed. She had got exactly what she wanted, and she had no intention of arriving in London wearing black, in which she always felt depressed.

She had gone instead to Edinburgh to stay with some rather dull friends she had made on her various trips who respected her for being self-effacing and very quiet in her appearance and had understood that she had no money to spend on herself.

The presents they had given her had been so enthusiastically received that both her host and hostess and a number of their friends had found themselves being unexpectedly generous to the "poor little widow."

Six months had passed quickly, and once Lily could be in half-mourning she shook the dust of Edinburgh from her feet and set off with a thrill of excitement to the South.

Lady Rushton received her with open arms.

The General was by this time practically bedridden, and she looked forward to the companionship of another woman, even one so much younger than herself.

What she had not expected was that Lily had no intention of sitting chatting or knitting by the fireside but was determined to storm Society.

By this time she had a very good idea of her own attractions.

Having no longer to act the part of being crushed by fate and perpetually on the verge of tears, she could hold her head high and demand the attention to which her lovely face entitled her.

She had spent every moment of her six months of mourning in learning all she could about the social life in which she intended to shine.

The story that Mrs. Langtry had captured first the attention of the artistic world by her beauty and finally the heart of the Prince had pointed for Lily the way to her own success.

She was not so foolish as to try to copy Mrs. Langtry in having only one black dress, but had decided she would dress entirely in white, which she knew with her red hair would look fantastic.

She was far too astute to pretend a sophistication she did not possess.

She had already learnt that everybody, men and

women, like to patronise somebody they thought was humble and subservient.

Lily flattered Lady Rushton by imploring her to help in finding her another husband.

"I am so stupid and untalented," she said sadly. "I know I ought to be able to earn a little money somehow, but as that seems impossible, I must find myself a man who is kind enough to ask me to be his wife."

"That should not be difficult," Lady Rushton said, looking at Lily's pleading eyes and white skin.

"Unfortunately, I know no young, unattached men," Lily went on, "and of course when we stayed in Edinburgh we were always with dear Ewan's friends—not that I would ever have looked at anybody but him!"

"I am afraid I have been rather remiss in not attending any parties since Alexander has been ill," Lady Rushton answered. "But now, for your sake, I must make an effort, and I am sure my friends will help me."

Because Sir Alexander had been an extremely distinguished soldier, it was not difficult for Lady Rushton to call on the wives of his brother-officers and arrange for Lily to be asked to Balls, parties, and Receptions.

Lily went on a shopping expedition and bought gowns that revealed her exquisite figure and bonnets which accentuated the colour of her hair.

Lady Rushton would have been very surprised if she had known how much Lily had in a secret Bank-account.

She had been systematically stealing from her husband ever since the first time he had been taken ill.

She did it so cleverly that he never suspected for an instant what was happening.

She had also insisted on having a Solicitor. He was young and impressionable, and when she told him wistfully that her elderly husband could leave her little money when he died, he was very helpful.

She offered to pay him, but instead he kissed her passionately before she left, and she enjoyed it.

On his advice, when Sir Ewan was dying she ran up huge bills in his name, which were the first call on the Estate when it was handed over to his son.

At every party men flocked to Lily's side, gazing at her with an undisguised admiration that was like sunshine breaking through the dark clouds after so many years of waiting.

Lily was wise enough to realise that for the moment women were more important than men, and she made herself so charming and again so pathetic that the Society matrons who might easily have closed their doors to her made sure that she was included in all their entertainments.

The Social World was a small one and the advent of a new face and a new beauty was passed from mouth to mouth from Belgravia to Mayfair, from Mayfair to St. James's.

Lily became a name to be mentioned in the same breath as the Professional Beauties such as Lady Randolph Churchill, Mrs. Cornwallis West, and Lady Dudley.

It was therefore inevitable that as she moved up the social ladder she should eventually meet the Prince of Wales.

At an afternoon Reception, acompanied by Lady Rushton, she was talking to somebody else when she heard a rather guttural voice ask:

"And how is your husband, Lady Rushton?"

She turned her head and saw her hostess sweeping to the ground in a low curtsey as she replied:

"A little better, Sire, and he will be very honoured that you have remembered to ask after him."

"Give him my kind regards and say I hope to see him at my next Reception."

Then the Prince of Wales's eyes were on Lily, and

she was well aware why he had crossed the room to speak to her sister-in-law.

When she curtseyed with a grace that she had practised for long hours in front of the mirror, she saw that flicker of admiration in his eyes that she had expected, and she was aware that he held her hand a little longer than was necessary.

As she went home with Lady Rushton she felt as if she were dancing on air, for she had received the invitation she coveted to Marlborough House, and she thought it was possible, indeed probable, that the Duke of Darleston might be there.

She had studied *Debrett* with great care, and she had also compiled a list in her mind of a number of eligible men who might become her husband.

There were not a great many.

It was fashionable for noblemen to be married off when they were young to some eminently suitable young woman, and, having provided an heir to their title and Estates, they could then enjoy themselves, as the Prince of Wales did, with the sophisticated beauties who, Lily thought scornfully, were waiting like cormorants for a fish.

She had no intention of joining their ranks. It was not a lover she wanted, but a husband, and a husband she intended to have.

When she met the Duke she knew that her choice, which she had made many years before, was an admirable one.

By this time she was aware that his love-affairs never lasted long, but she told herself she would marry him before he grew bored, and what he did after that would not be important.

When she was in Edinburgh it had been fashionable amongst the younger women to visit a Fortune-Teller.

"She is uncanny," one of her friends had told her.

"She can see things in one's past that are so secret that one has never breathed them to a living soul."

"But what about the future?" Lily had asked.

"She is infallible! Every word she says comes true!"

Lily had visited Mrs. McDonald in a back street where she received her customers.

She was an elderly Scottish woman who looked "fey" and undoubtedly had some clairvoyant ability, but Lily decided she made up what she could not "see."

At the same time, Mrs. McDonald reiterated over and over again that she had a great future in front of her.

"Ye'll walk with th' greatest in th' land," she said, rolling her *R*'s which made what she said more impressive than it might have sounded otherwise. "Ye'll glitter with jewels like a Queen, an' there'll be men, always men tae acclaim yer beauty."

She elaborated on this prophecy a little, then asked:

"Have ye a question tae ask me?"

Lily shook her head.

"I think not," she replied. "You have told me all I want to know."

The old woman looked surprised.

"Wot aboot love? Theer's nay a lassie comes here as does nae wish tae talk aboot love."

Lily smiled and she went on:

"Noo look, ma dear, hearrts will be thrown at yer feet, but ye'll gie yer own, sooner or later, an' there'll be nae takin' it back."

She shut her eyes in concentration before she said:

"Noo yer heed rules yer hearrt, bu' one day yer hearrt'll win th' battle, an' ye'll find oot which is th' strongest."

The old woman looked at her.

"Remember all Ah've told ye, an' for what ye've set oot tae do, ye'll need all yer wits aboot ye."

"I will remember," Lily replied in an uninterested voice.

She put a half-guinea down on the table, thinking as she did so that it was a lot of money to spend on what her brain told her was really thought-reading, but at the same time it contributed to her self-assurance.

Now as she came down the stairs from the Second Floor to the large Drawing-Room which overlooked the trees in Belgrave Square, she told herself that every-thing she had planned and had worked for was coming true.

The Duke of Darleston was waiting for her and she was determined, with a cast-iron determination that had driven her to get what she wanted since she was fifteen, that he would be her husband.

The Fortune-Teller in Edinburgh had made Lily think of another way in which she could help herself.

If an old woman living in the back street could sense things about people in a way which the Scots called "fey," she was quite certain it was a power that everybody could use.

She thought it was just a question of developing it, and she had lived in Scotland for long enough to know that in every village there was some old body who was consulted about the future because she had what people called "second sight."

To Lily it was a gift which she thought she could use to further her ambitions.

If she could sense what a man was feeling and think-ing, then her power over him would be even more effec-tive than if he was just beguiled by her beauty.

She trained herself to try to see perceptively into the minds of almost everybody she met, and she thought that on a number of occasions she had been extremely successful.

At any rate it made her find out quickly what were a man's habits and interests.

Where women were concerned she had usually encouraged them to speak of their sensitivity and perhaps a secret unhappiness, and they would confide in her in a manner which certainly gave her an insight into their frustrations and miseries.

Now she told herself that if she was to captivate and hold the Duke, she must from the very beginning make him realise that she was different from all the other women with whom he had associated and of whom she had learnt he tried remarkably quickly.

She went to the Drawing-Room door.

The Duke, looking very attractive and extremely raffish, was standing amongst the old-fashioned furniture and seeming to dominate the whole room.

She stood for a moment in the doorway, conscious that with her white gown and her red hair, fortunately dressed only that morning by the hairdresser, she looked very lovely.

Her eyes were round with astonishment before she moved towards him.

"This is a surprise, Your Grace," she said, "and I regret to tell you that my sister-in-law is not at home."

"I came to see you," the Duke replied.

He took her hand in his and held it for a moment while he looked into her eyes, before he raised it to his lips.

"To see me?" Lily asked ingenuously.

"I think you are as aware as I was that we had not finished our conversation last evening at Marlborough House. In fact, His Royal Highness interrupted us to sweep you away from me, and I hoped you would be aware that I had not even begun what I wished to say."

It was not only what the Duke said which Lily found so enlightening, but the fact that his eyes were, she knew taking in every facet of her face and the sweep of her long eye-lashes, and she dropped them rather shyly, as if his admiration embarrassed her.

She took her hand from his and he said:

"Come and sit down. I have an invitation to offer you which I hope you will accept."

She did not answer, but she thought that an invitation to Darle Castle was exactly what she wanted.

It would give her the chance to see the house that one day would be hers, where she would act as hostess to the whole of the Social World.

She gave him a faint smile that was a little unsure and a little questioning, as if she was not certain what his invitation would be and was already wondering how she could accept it.

She sat down on the sofa, siting upright with her hands clasped in her lap and her face turned towards the Duke.

As she sat, she knew that her hair would be haloed by the pale winter sunshine coming in through the window behind her.

"I have decided," the Duke said, "to leave almost immediately for Egypt in my yacht, and I hope that you will join me as one of my guests."

"To Egypt?" Lily questioned.

This was something she had certainly not expected, and, being unprepared, she was not quite certain how she should reply.

At the same time, she knew with a leap of her heart that if she was alone with the Duke in his yacht on such a long voyage, it would be impossible for him to escape from her.

As she looked at the sun that had no warmth in it, the Duke said:

"I want to travel up the Nile, and I only learnt this morning for the first time that it never rains in Egypt!"

He laughed as he spoke, and Lily thought it made him even more attractive than he was before.

"You will come?" he asked.

She did not reply, and after a moment he went on:

"I have asked Lord and Lady Southwold, of whom you may have heard, and two men, James Bushly and a very old friend of mine, Harry Settingham, whom you met last evening at Marlborough House."

"Yes, of course!" Lily said.

"We will be six," the Duke said, "and I think I can promise you, Lady Cairns, a very happy and a very comfortable voyage."

There was a little pause, then Lily rose to her feet to walk to one of the windows and look out at the Square.

The sun had just disappeared behind a cloud and in consequence everything looked drab and grey and wintry.

The Duke had risen when she did but he was still on the hearth-rug, watching her and waiting for her to speak.

"I—I do not know what to—say," Lily said hesitatingly.

"What is the problem?" he enquired.

"I am still in—half-mourning," Lily replied, "and I feel perhaps it would be—wrong to enjoy myself so much as I would with you when I am still—missing my dear—husband."

As she spoke she thought she had said it well and in a voice that any man would find extremely moving.

"I think what you need," the Duke said, "is a holiday away from the past, if you like, with new faces and new people to occupy your mind."

"You make it sound very fascinating," Lily said without turning her head.

"That is what I want it to be," he said, "and because I know what is best for you, I do not intend to take 'no' for an answer."

She turned round then and there was a smile on her lips.

"I—I hope it is the—right thing for—me—to do."

She thought he was waiting for an explanation, and she went on:

"My husband was a very autocratic and authoritative man. I am not—used to making—decisions for myself."

"Then I will certainly make them for you," the Duke replied. "Can you be ready the day after tomorrow?"

She moved from the window towards him.

"I suppose if you tell me so—I shall have to be."

"Then that is an order!" he said. "And your brother-in-law will tell you, if you ask him, that orders have to be obeyed!"

"I will be—ready!" Lily said meekly.

"I cannot tell you how happy you have made me!"

She raised her eyes to his.

"That is what I want to do—make you happy—but I am told that happiness is what you give other people."

"That is the sort of compliment I like to hear," the Duke said with a smile.

He continued to look into her eyes, and once again Lily's lashes, which were a little darker than nature intended, were silhouetted against her white skin.

Then she settled herself down on the sofa again and the Duke said:

"I have decided that as the Bay of Biscay can be very unpleasant at this time of the year, we will go overland and join my yacht at Marseilles. *The Mermaid* has in fact already left harbour and is on her way."

"*The Mermaid?*" Lily repeated. "What a lovely name, and so very—romantic."

"That is what I thought when I christened her. Do you play Bridge?"

"Yes—yes, of course!" Lily replied.

She was glad now that she had paid for lessons while she was in Edinburgh, knowing that Bridge was the latest craze, although the Duchess of Devonshire insisted on playing the old-fashioned Whist.

"There will be plenty to amuse us if it is too cold to be on deck," the Duke remarked, "but once we reach Egypt I am certain you will be as entranced by the Temples as I shall."

For a moment Lily wondered what the Temples in Egypt would be like.

She had never met anybody who was in the least interested in that far-away country, and although she had been taught about the Pyramids and the Sphinx, she had always somehow connected Temples with India rather than with Egypt.

"It will certainly be—fascinating," she said.

"I have sent my Comptroller," the Duke went on, "to purchase every book on Egypt that is obtainable from the Libraries, and we can spend some of the time when we are in the Mediterranean finding out about the Pharaohs."

"And of course Cleopatra," Lily said, remembering that she had been a beauty like herself.

"I shall not want to look at her when you are there," the Duke said.

Lily was not certain whether the words came automatically from long practice.

At the same time, there was no doubt from the expression in his eyes that he was finding her as beautiful as she believed herself to be.

Before he left she said hesitatingly:

"You are—quite, quite sure you want me to—come with you? After all, Your Grace—since I have lived so long in the North, you may find me—rather dull, and very—ignorant about the things that—interest you."

"I will tell you exactly what interests me when we have more time," the Duke replied.

He kissed her hand again on leaving, and only when the door of the Drawing-Room shut behind him did Lily turn to the looking-glass over the mantelpiece to stare at her reflection.

She thought as she did so that it would be impossible for any woman to look lovelier or indeed more fascinating.

"I am beautiful, and already he wants me!" she said beneath her breath. "But I have to play my cards very, very carefully if he is to offer me mariage, as I intend him to do.'

She resisted an impulse to go to the window and watch the Duke drive away in his carriage which had been waiting across the Square.

Nevertheless, she sent her thoughts after him, saying:

"You are mind! My husband! Mine!"

Then the intensity of them turned to a cry of sheer delight and triumph.

"Egypt!" she cried, and flung her hands high in the air. "Egypt! And there will be no other distractions besides me!"

Chapter Three

Travelling across France in the Duke's private rail-way-carriage, which was attached to the Express to Marseilles, Lily thought that the luxury and the comfort were beyond anything she could have imagined.

'This is what it means to be really rich!' she thought with satisfaction.

She thought that when she married the Duke she would feel as if she floated on a golden cloud and that the stars were made of diamonds.

It was impossible not to feel romantic when she looked at him, while at the same time his attractions were framed and gilded by his possessions.

Almost every conversation told her more about the wonders of Darle Castle and what the Duke owned in other parts of the country.

But apart from him, Lily found that all the other

guests lived a life of luxury that was very different from her life with Sir Ewan.

Lady Southwold was the only other woman, and Lily had been a little apprehensive as to what she would be like.

They had met first in the Drawing-Room compartment of the train at Victoria, and a first glance told Lily that she was well over thirty and there was no reason for her to fear any competition from Amy Southwold.

Then when the journey started, she found that although Lady Southwold might not be beautiful, she had an unmistakable fascination and was also extremely witty and amusing.

This actually was the reason why the Duke had invited her and her husband, with Harry's full approval, to join the party.

Lord Southwold, who had only recently been raised to the Peerage, thanks to his friendship with the Prince of Wales, was an extremely intelligent man who had inherited one fortune, then doubled and trebled it by his own expertise.

Those who invariably criticised the Prince of Wales hinted that Lord Southwold was one of the Financiers who helped him invest his money and took particular care that he did not lose it.

That put him in the same group as the Rothschilds, but everybody who knew Charles Southwold liked him, and although he was older than the Duke and Harry, they counted him as one of their closest friends.

Amy had laughed her way into Society and the Duke knew that she could always be relied on to make any party, however heavy, a success.

When he had invited her to come with him to Egypt she had exclaimed:

"Oh, Dasher, you are the answer to my prayers, as

you have been before! Charlie has been over-working lately and I was wondering where we should go so that he would be able to do nothing but eat, drink, and enjoy the sunshine."

"That is exactly what he can do on *The Mermaid*," the Duke had replied.

"He will love being with you and Harry, and so shall I," Amy Southwold had said. "You are not only the most attractive man I know, but also the kindest."

"You are embarrassing me," the Duke had replied, "but I also want to get away to the sunshine, and I am very grateful to you and Charlie for accompanying me."

Amy was certain that his insistence on leaving was due to the rumour, which of course had reached her ears, that his affair with Myrtle was over, but when she saw Lily she thought there was obviously a new reason as well.

The Duke's fourth guest, James Bushly, had been in the Regiment with him and was a perfect guest in every house-party, so that hostesses fought to include him and those who were unkind said that he had so many beds to choose from that he had no time to fill his own with a wife.

He often said that he, the Duke, and Harry were the "Three Musketeers."

"Three bachelors in search of adventure!" he elaborated. "And so far I do not remember our ever being disappointed."

Jimmy Bushly's love-affairs lasted longer than the Duke's, but he still evaded with some dexterity the traps set for him by ambitious Mamas.

He was likely one day to become the Earl of Thame, if the present holder of the title did not produce an heir, which appeared to be unlikely, and when his father, a comparatively young man, died.

However, his future prospects did not worry Jimmy, although they were duly noted by the Social World.

Like the Duke he always said that he had no intention of marrying, and like the Duke he always received the answer that sooner or later he would have to produce an heir.

In the meantime, he enjoyed life, and although he had not the intelligence of The Dasher, he was an excellent audience and could always be relied upon to take part in any activity in which the Duke was particularly interested.

When Jimmy saw Lily, there was a twisted smile at the corners of his mouth, and he said to Harry in a voice that only he could hear:

"Now I understand the rush to leave England!"

Harry's eyes twinkled but he did not reply.

He was thinking that Lily was undoubtedly one of the loveliest women he had ever seen, and because he was so fond of the Duke, he only hoped the inside of the parcel was as attractive as the outside.

Once they reached Calais and the Duke's private coach was attached to the Express, they all settled down as if prepared to make a "home away from home" wherever they might find themselves.

The food which was served by the Duke's servants was superb because it was cooked by one of the Duke's Chefs, the wines were outstanding, and Lily was to sleep in a large, comfortable bed made up with linen bearing the Duke's coronet.

She told herself it would be like having a *genie* who could magically produce everything one could wish for.

She could not help wondering how soon the Duke would approach her as a lover.

She was considering whether she should look shocked and say that she could not contemplate any liaison which did not involve a wedding-ring.

Then she told herself that in that case she might frighten him off from the very beginning.

She was not a young girl whom he would think it wrong to seduce, but a widow who was, in the parlance of the Clubs, "fair game."

Having seen the rest of the party, Lily was well aware of the part the Duke expected her to play and that she was to be the main factor in keeping him amused.

At the same time, unlike any other man she had known, he enjoyed life so tremendously that he was the one who stimulated the laughter and who encouraged Amy Southwold to be witty with words as sharp as pointed arrows. To listen to him sparring verbally with Harry and Jimmy was almost like watching a performance on the stage.

It made Lily realise that only an exceptional woman could keep up with the rest, and she knew that first evening that with her limited knowledge of the life the other guests lived, she had no chance of being the star when they were all together.

She thought things over and decided she could hold the Duke simply by her beauty, and hoped that as there would be no competition, he would concentrate on her until she knew him well enough to enslave him.

She had it all worked out in her mind, and as they travelled through France she was aware that his desire for her was growing and she saw by the expression in his eyes that it would not be long before he made a move.

She expected it would happen when they reached the yacht at Marseilles.

Having listened attentively to everything everybody was saying, she tentatively tried a new approach which she had formulated in her mind.

It was at dinner that she said to Lord Southwold:

"Do you use your instinct when you are buying shares on the Stock Exchange?"

"My instinct?" he repeated. "No, not often, although I sometimes have what you might call a 'hunch.' "

"That is what I meant."

"And your 'hunches' certainly pay off, Charles!" Harry said with a laugh.

"I was once told about a man," Lily said, "who made a fortune because he followed the signs of the stars."

"How interesting!" Amy exclaimed. "But how did he do that?"

"An Astrologer worked it all out for him."

"The Egyptians believed in Astrology," the Duke said. "In fact the Pharaohs did little without consulting the Palace Astrologers, who, from all I can ascertain, were kept very busy."

"I wonder if we will find one there now?" Amy questioned.

"I am quite certain there will be a horde of charlatans only too willing to tell your fortune," Harry said. "Everybody who comes back from India says the 'Gully-Gully' men in Alexandria are a perfect nuisance, besides being cruel to the chickens they use in their prognostications."

"I did not mean that sort of thing!" Lily protested. "I was thinking really of people who are 'fey,' like the Scottish."

"But of course! They can really 'see,' " Amy agreed.

"Yes—I know!" Lily said in a low voice.

The way she spoke made Charles Southwold look at her sharply.

"Are you telling us," he asked, "that you are 'fey'?"

"Sometimes. It always seems incredible at first, but eventually things come true, and it surprises me as much as it does everybody else!"

"Well, I must certainly ask you to use your power on my behalf," Charles Southwold said. "I have three deals in question at the moment, and I should be very inter-

ested to hear any advice as to whether or not they are
likely to be a success or a failure."

"I will—try to tell—you," Lily said a little shyly.

Amy gave a cry of excitement.

"But this is fascinating! Of course you must tell us
all what we shall find in the future."

"Now you are frightening me!" Lily protested. "If I
tell you that something is wrong, you may be angry, or
even leave me stranded in the desert while you steam
away!"

"I promise you that is very unlikely," the Duke said.

Lily saw the expression in his eyes and felt her excitement grow.

He wanted her. There was no doubt about that, and
in her plan to make him interested not only in her face
but in something mysterious and elusive, she felt quite
certain that she was on the right track.

Marseilles was bathed in sunshine but there was a
nip in the wind and at night darkness came early.

The Mermaid was larger and more impressive than
Lily had imagined it would be. It was the Duke's latest
acquisition and he was very proud of it.

What was more, it was, with the exception of the
Royal Yacht, the largest yacht in the private possession of
any British citizen, and he had supervised the building
of it so that in a way it was more exclusively his than
were any of the houses he had inherited.

Every gadget ever invented had been incorporated,
and the decorations, chosen by the Politician's wife, who
had extremely good taste, were very attractive.

The stewards were augmented by some of the Duke's
personal servants who travelled with him, and his Chef
took over the Galley.

Lily found with a little smile of satisfaction that her
very large and comfortable cabin was next to the Master
Suite, which was what she had expected.

The first night they did not move from the harbour and dinner was a very enjoyable meal, with Lady South-wold and Lily dressed in their prettiest evening-gowns with jewels flashing on their bare necks.

They talked for a long time at the dinner-table, and when they moved from the Dining-Saloon into another extremely comfortable Saloon, Lady Southwold said:

"I hope, Lady Cairns, you will show us tonight some of your powers of 'second sight.' At least it is quiet and peaceful here."

On the train when they had asked her to tell their fortunes, Lily had made the excuse that the rumble of the wheels was too disturbing and the movement made it difficult to concentrate.

Now she smiled and said:

"I will certainly try, but I wish I had not mentioned it in the first place. I have always found that clairvoyance is not something you can order or perform at will. It has to come to one like a shaft of moonlight, and is impossi-ble to control."

While they were talking, the gentlemen joined them and Amy Southwold said:

"It is so exciting! Lady Cairns says she will try her powers tonight. I know it is something which will really interest us all."

"Do you need any 'props' for your exhibition?" Har-ry enquired.

There was something in the way he spoke and in the laughter in his eyes which made Lily suspect that he thought what she was doing was designed to draw atten-tion to herself.

But what he thought or did not think was unimportant, and as she looked at the Duke a little pleadingly he said:

"You must not let Harry tease you. I am sure being 'fey' is to you something serious and not to be treated lightly."

"You—understand," she said.

"I want to."

For a moment she looked into his eyes and the rest of the party was forgotten.

Then as if she felt she must prove herself she said:

"It is easier if I have something with which to concentrate, and the same applies to whomever I am helping."

"What do you need?" the Duke asked.

"It is unlikely that you have a crystal ball on board," Lily answered, "so a pack of cards will do."

After she had been to Mrs. McDonald in Edinburgh she had searched the Libraries for books on clairvoyance and Fortune-Telling, and to her surprise she had found quite a number, most of which she thought were rubbish.

At the same time, they told her what she wanted to learn, which was what each card was supposed to predict. She learnt, however, that what had been used through the centuries for more advanced clairvoyance was the Tarot-cards.

As these seemed rather complicated, she decided that playing-cards were something with which she could show off her hands while using what she called her "instinct" to tell the person who was consulting her what they wished to know.

She was certain that imagination was the secret of Mrs. McDonald's success, and she had also collected every possible detail from Lady Rushton about the Duke's friends before they had left London.

Unfortunately there had not been much time, but she had also looked them up in *Debrett* and the night before she left for Egypt was at a dinner-party where fortunately she was seated next to a well-known gossip.

When she told him she was to be a guest of the

Duke of Darleston and who were to be the other guests, he told her a great many things she was certain would now come in useful.

"I will try to consult the fates for Lord Southwold," she said, "but only if he promises that if he loses money as a result of my advice, he will not expect me to make good any deficiency in his Bank-account!"

There was laughter over this and Harry remarked:

"If Charles loses money, he puts it down to experience, and that is what you will undoubtedly give him, Lady Cairns."

The Duke brought Lily a pack of new cards and she seated herself at a card-table.

Then she said:

"I think it would be embarrassing if you are all listening, and besides you will laugh and disturb my train of thought. Could the rest of you play Bridge and forget Lord Southwold and me?"

"A good idea!" the Duke commended. "Lady Cairns can take us one by one when we are sitting out, and afterwards we can repeat the less personal revelations!"

There was a good deal of laughter and Jimmy said:

"If Lady Cairns has any revelations to make about The Dasher, it will undoubtedly take all night—in which case he had better be last!"

They all agreed to this, and as the others seated themselves at another card-table which a steward erected for them, Lily opened the pack of cards she held in her hand, shuffled them, and held them out to Lord Southwold.

"Do you really think these are necessary?" he asked.

"As I have said, they are helpful," she said, "but I do not need these cards to know that you yourself have a strong, very clear intuition which you must never deny."

She made a quick sketch of his character, which, as it was extremely flattering, he made no effort to contradict. She then managed to make an intelligent guess about the propositions of which he had spoken.

"Two," she said, "will turn out to be all you expect of them, but beware of one which appears extremely attractive but is fundamentally unsound."

She gave him a beguiling smile as she said:

"It seems unnecessary to say this to you, and I am sure you are so clever you know already where there is something wrong, and that you judge your investments as you judge people."

"What do you mean by that?" he asked.

"I think you have an analytical mind," she replied, "and it would be very difficult, in fact almost impossible, for a person whom you knew well to deceive you. You merely extend that knowledge when you deal with stocks and shares."

"I believe you are right!" Lord Southwold said reflectively.

"I am sure I am," Lily answered. "Because in many ways you are very modest about your own brilliance, you think that what happens in business is just the reward of efficiency, when actually it is so much more."

By the time the first hand had finished at the other table and Harry, who was dummy in the second hand, crossed to where Lily was still talking to Lord Southwold, she was aware that she had achieved her first success.

"You are a very clever woman!" Charles Southwold said as he rose somewhat reluctantly from his seat opposite her. "They say Napoleon never moved without consulting an Astrologer and several Fortune-Tellers, and I am tempted to ask you to join my staff."

"Be careful," Lily warned. "I might accept!"

Harry sat down opposite her and she knew that he was unimpressed and she thought, although she could not be sure, a little hostile.

She made him shuffle the cards, then picked out twelve of them which she arranged in a pattern with one, which represented himself, in the centre.

Then she said:

"It is very difficult to tell you, because you have erected a barrier round yourself. Tonight I shall not attempt to climb it, but wait until you open the door to me, which is at present closed."

"Are you saying that you have nothing to say to me?" Harry asked.

"Yes, Mr. Settingham," Lily replied, "for reasons I have just explained."

"A barrier? What barrier?"

"That is for you to say. I only know it is there."

She looked at him across the table and felt as if he was sizing her up like a duellist calculating the dexterity of his opponent.

Then he smiled.

I hope you will be kind to me another evening," he said. "But I realise that an unbeliever always causes trouble."

"Invariably!" Lily agreed.

Harry rose and Lady Southwold exclaimed:

"You cannot have finished already! Or has Lady Cairns nothing to tell you?"

"She turned me away from the temple of knowledge," Harry replied lightly. "She says I am an 'unbeliever.'"

"Then I shall take your place," the Duke said. "Personally, I am prepared to believe anything Lady Cairns tells me!"

Without arguing, he sat down in the seat which Harry had just vacated.

Because they knew he expected it, the others went on with their Bridge, talking amongst themselves, and the Duke said in a low voice:

"Only you can tell me if the future holds what I want more than anything else."

"Will you shuffle the cards, Your Grace?"

"There is no need for cards," he said. "Look at me, Lily, and tell me the answer to my problem, which quite simply I hope is . . . 'yes'!"

She did not pretend to misunderstand what he was saying, she only looked across the table into his eyes and felt the excitement within herself rising until she felt it overwhelmed her.

It was impossible not to be aware of the light in his eyes and the invitation on his lips.

He was the Duke of Darleston, the man she had thought about and dreamt about for years, the man whom she intended to marry.

Because her astute mind told her it would be a mistake to surrender too easily, she said:

"Have you ever dreamt that you were standing on a very high mountain or on the top of a lofty tower and you wonder whether if you jump you will fall crashing to the ground, or by some miracle be carried safely on wings?"

"Do you mean the wings are there if you desire to use them?"

"Yes."

"Then you will not be flying alone."

His voice was soft and beguiling and, Lily thought, irresistible.

"I want you to answer me, Lily," he said.

She looked at him without speaking and he added:

"The question is no longer there, and to save you from giving me the answer, I will make it for you."

"Thank—you," Lily whispered.

* * *

Later that night, when she lay in his arms, she told herself that it was easy to think she had won the battle, but she had a long way to go before she was victorious.

The Duke had exclaimed over her beauty, she knew she excited him, but she was well aware that the question of marriage had not entered his mind.

She had also learnt at the party her last night in London that it was a surprise that Lady Garforth was not going to Egypt.

"Did I hear you say Egypt?" she heard her remark to Lady Rushton. "Good Heavens! Why on earth should Darleston want to go there?"

"It is not a bad idea to seek the sun in this weather," a man said. "Who is going with him?"

"My sister-in-law, for one," Lady Rushton replied.

"Your sister-in-law?"

The first speaker seemed astounded. Then he had said:

"But I thought Lady Garfor . . ."

He realised he was being indiscreet and bit back the words, but Lily knew what he had intended to say.

She remembered then that Lady Garforth had been at the Duke's side when they were at Marlborough House.

There had been another man with them but Lily had noticed the expression in Lady Garforth's eyes when she looked at the Duke, and although it had meant nothing particular at the time, she remembered it now.

So it was she with whom he had been associating before he had met her!

On the way back from the party she had learnt that Lady Garforth was a widow like herself, and there was therefore no reason why the Duke, if he wished to do so, should not marry her.

'I must be careful! Very careful!' she thought.

But it was difficult to think when the Duke's lips were seeking hers, his hands were touching her body, and she knew that the women who had said he was a fascinating, exciting lover had told the truth.

As Lily put her arms round his neck to draw him closer still, she told herself fiercely that she would never let him go and would make it impossible for him to escape her.

*   *   *

The following day they were in the Mediterranean and the Duke made it very clear to the rest of the party to whom he wanted to talk.

He took Lily up on the bridge and walked with her on the deck, and she joined him in his private cabin where none of his guests ventured unless they were particularly invited.

"You are beautiful!" he said to her. "I was wise to bring you away from London before you were spoilt by the adoration which sooner or later is bound to turn your head!"

"I deserve it!" Lily replied. "Although the grouse, the eagles, and the blackbirds may admire me, they are not very articulate in saying so."

"I will make up for them," the Duke answered.

He pulled her into his arms and kissed her until she felt dizzy with the joy of it.

"I do not believe Cleopatra could have been any lovelier than you," he said the next day.

Once again they were in his private cabin, and she was leisurely turning over the books he had been reading about Egypt.

"I am glad she is dead."

"Why?" the Duke enquired.

"Because otherwise you would prefer her to me. After all, what man could resist a Queen and one who could offer him all the mysteries of Egypt?"

"I am quite content with your mysteries."

"I have not yet told you about yourself."

"I have no wish to know the future," the Duke said. "If you told me what races I was going to win they would lose their excitement, and also it is distinctly unsportsmanlike to bet on a certainty."

"I am not thinking of races."

"Then what?"

"Of you, of your feelings and your emotions."

"That is quite easy," the Duke said. "I do not need cards to know that you excite me, and all I am concerned with at the moment is exciting you."

He kissed her again, and it was impossible to go on talking and Lily told herself there was no point in it now.

But the others were not put off so easily.

Lady Southwold insisted upon having her fortune told, and so did James Bushly, while Lord Southwold continued to sing her praises as being extraordinarily accurate and astute.

When he had a chance to speak to Lily alone, he said:

"I want to use your 'second sight' again, but at the moment our host appears to have made a 'take-over bid' in a big way."

"I always have time for you, Lord Southwold."

"Thank you for saying that," he replied. "I am well aware that I must take my turn."

She smiled at him beguilingly, and he said:

"I have a deal in mind on which I want your advice, or rather, to use your 'eye.' If it comes off, you shall tell me which are your favourite stones, which I imagine are emeralds."

"They are my birth-stone," Lily said softly.

"Then I think it is time you had a birthday."

Lily shut her eyes for a moment. Then she said:

"I think you ought to go ahead with what you are planning, but cautiously. There is one man whom I do not trust. You should consider everything he suggests to you very, very carefully. Weigh it up and use your own intuition, which I have told you is unusually perceptive, before you make any move, however hard he may try to persuade you."

She paused, and although she did not open her eyes she knew that Lord Southwold was watching her intently.

"What else can you see?" he asked at length.

"I see you attaining everything you desire. Failure is impossible. You are omnipotent and infallible, but at the same time—be cautious!"

"That is exactly what I felt myself," Lord Southwold remarked, and Lily, opening her eyes, thought it was all too easy.

The only person in the party who did not show an almost abject respect for her powers as a "Seer" was Harry.

When she met his eyes across the table at meals and when Lord Southwold spoke of her powers with a note of reverence, she was aware that Harry was not deceived.

She felt somehow as if he could, if he wished, expose her as a cheat, a charlatan, and a fraud.

Then she told herself that she was being ridiculous and needlessly apprehensive.

She had not done or said anything wrong, she had merely planted in people who had an almost childish belief in good luck the idea that she could see their future.

As far as she was concerned, that could not be anything but the primrose path and the crock of gold at the end of the rainbow.

"They are so rich, they are so important," Lily told herself when she was alone in her cabin. "It makes them safe from poverty, loneliness, and fear."

She felt a little shudder go through her as she remembered how poor she and her father had been, and she remembered too how nervous she had been of the

future as she realised that Sir Ewan was likely to die and
how little money he could leave her.

She had certainly improved the situation once he
was tied to his bed, by going round the Castle collecting
everything that was not likely to be entailed and sending
it to Edinburgh.

When she had been staying there with her husband's
relatives she had made contact with a man who dealt in
antiques.

She had told him a long and complicated story of
being left by her family a large number of small objects
which they wanted her to keep and treasure for senti-
mental reasons, but which she had found an encumbrance.

"I could not bear to hurt them after all their kind-
ness," she said, looking pathetic and speaking in her
childish voice. "But because I am desperately in need of
money, I must sell something from time to time, but of
course the transactions must be kept entirely secret."

"I understand," the Dealer replied, "and I promise
you, anything you sell me will be conveyed as quickly as
possible to a shop I have in London."

Lily sent him some snuff-boxes which fetched a
surprisingly large sum, small items of table-silver from
the safe which she thought would not be missed as they
were unable to entertain, and even a few small and mi-
nor paintings that she could not find included in the
catalogue which listed the contents of the house.

When Sir Ewan was dead and she went to stay in
Edinburgh, she sold his gold watch and chain, several
pairs of his cuff-links, and some very fine pearl studs that
he always wore in the evening.

Alister had actually asked her what had happened to
them.

"I have no idea," she answered, "but your father's
old valet died five years ago, and he did not like the man

he engaged to succeed him, so when he left he preferred to be looked after by the Butler and the footman."

Alister Cairns had pursed his lips into a hard line.

"I suppose it is no use asking the Police to make enquiries about the man?"

"He told me when he left that he intended to go to Australia," Lily replied. "He said he had relatives there."

She knew that Alister was not likely to pursue the matter further, and the money went into her secret account at the Bank, which she had transferred to London as soon as she went South, still using the fictitious name that she had used in Scotland.

Yet, whatever she had accumulated, by fair means or foul, was a mere drop in the ocean compared to the great fortunes enjoyed by the Duke, Lord Southwold, and, as far as she could make out, the majority of their friends.

Harry was teased by Lady Southwold as being a "rich bachelor who spent money on nobody but himself," and Jimmy, although he did not appear to have much money at the moment, obviously had big expectations.

They made Lily feel as if she had stepped into an Aladdin's cave and everything round her glittered blindingly, especially the Duke. She felt as if his strong, athletic body shimmered with gems and his coronet was ablaze with them.

'That is what I want on my head,' Lily thought.

She had a picture of herself moving amongst the Peeresses, a huge tiara on her red hair, a necklace of diamonds encircling her white throat, and her bracelets shining dazzlingly with every move she made.

"The Duchess of Darleston!" That was what she would be, and besides having the title she would be married to the most alluring, most fascinating man she had ever imagined.

Then she was suddenly aware that there was another adjective that was often used when people spoke of him—the most raffish!

As she waited for him to come through the door of her cabin, she was afraid that after all her calculations her heart might betray her!

Chapter Four

The Duke stood on deck alone.

It was very early in the morning, and the sun rising in the cloud-free, mist-free sky threw a strange, mystical light, first red, then yellow, lastly a blinding white, over the landscape.

"No wonder," he thought, "the ancient Egyptians worshipped, above all other Deities, the God of the Sun."

Every mile they travelled since they had left the Mediterranean for first the Nile Delta, which was like a lotus, and then the river itself, he had felt more and more fascinated by the country he wished to see.

Now the river moved through mile after mile of green, with cotton and tobacco fields, palm groves, and plantations of beans and peas springing from the rich, red-brown mud. In the distance, waterless and sun-dried, was the golden desert.

As they went farther South, the river itself was

surprisingly empty. Sometimes the Duke would see the lateen sail of a felucca and an occasional barge moving slowly through the brown water, but otherwise there were only the birds.

But the view was often of mud-built villages with their flat roofs shafted by palm trees, patient plodding donkeys carrying huge loads, and men in long white galabiehs labouring in the fields.

They used hoes and dibbers which the Duke thought were the same shape and type that their ancestors had used over five thousand years earlier.

He was intensely interested in the creaking, groaning Shaduf, or water-pump, a primitive apparatus of water-buckets attached to a vertical wheel and operated by a circular wooden treadmill round which oxen or donkeys endlessly revolved.

But what really thrilled him was that soon he would have a sight of the Temples and the statues which had been left by the Pharaohs at Thebes.

He could not explain to himself why he was so intrigued or why he felt a new and very different excitement from anything he had ever known before. It was almost, he felt, as if there was a familiarity not only about what he saw but what he felt about the country.

It was this which made him resist the pleading of his party that they should make a stop at Cairo and enjoy the gaieties of belly-dancers and other exotic entertainments instead of pressing on toward Luxor.

There had been a brief glimpse of the great Pyramids, but the Duke refused to change his plans.

Only Amy Southwold had been delighted with his decision, because it meant that Charles would continue to take things easy and spend most of the time on deck under the awning, reading or sleeping.

He roused himself in the evenings to join in the laughter and chatter at dinner, and he insisted that Lily should use her "eye" to look into the future of his financial operations.

"I only hope she has a stake in the great fortune she is making for you!" the Duke had said. "But take warning, Charlie, when you look round you, note that even the greatest Empires can crumble away and leave nothing but rocks and stones behind them!"

"It will be a long time," Lily said in an intense voice, "before Lord Southwold's Empire vanishes. In fact it has not yet reached its zenith."

She found that when she spoke in a certain voice, with her eyes misty and vacant as if she looked into the future, Lord Southwold listened to her raptly, and the others seemed impressed.

As far as the Duke was concerned, she was so beautiful that it did not matter to him what she said, for he liked the movements of her lips because they were kissable rather than because they mouthed prophecies which only time could prove to be right or wrong.

Although Lily tried to pretend that she understood his desire to move South without lingering on the way, she privately thought it a pity that they did not have a chance to visit the shops in Cairo, especially those which sold jewellery.

Lord Southwold had referred several times to his promise to give her emeralds, and the Duke, realising how little jewellery she had and that what she did wear was very inferior to the necklaces, earrings, and bracelets which adorned Lady Southwold, had promised her diamonds to echo the light in her eyes.

"I cannot imagine why you should be so beautiful," he said more than once. "What did you mother look like?"

Lily felt a touch of fear as she thought how horrified he would be if she told him the truth. Instead she said sadly:

"Alas, I cannot remember. She died soon after I was born, but my father always said she was very lovely."

"Then you must be like her," the Duke said. "But as your father was an Englishman, how did you meet your husband?"

"My father always went to Scotland for the grouse-shooting," Lily replied, "and when I was seventeen he took me with him. My husband always said that he fell in love with me the moment he saw me."

"That is not surprising."

"He was a Chieftain and he appeared very romantic."

"He was very much older than you," the Duke commented.

"Much older, and I suppose in a way he was a father-figure, which means I had never—loved anybody—properly—until I met—you."

The way she spoke with a little hesitation over the word "properly" made the Duke's lips seek hers, and to her relief there was no further conversation about her past.

She knew, however, that it was extremely important, if she was to be a Duchess, to establish the fact that her antecedents were impeccable, for she knew that the Duke would be unwilling to marry beneath him.

She therefore invented a number of distinguished relatives who were of course dead, and who when they were alive had lived in obscure parts of the British Isles so that the Duke and his friends were not likely to have heard of them.

"My mother's family was always supposed to be descended from the Kings of Ireland," she said once at the dinner-table, "which caused an endless conflict with my husband, who believed the Cairns are descended from one of the Kings of Scotland."

"It is not surprising that you are 'fey'!" Lord Southwold

remarked. "A mixture of Irish and Scottish is bound to have an explosive quality about it!"

"Which is certainly true when you drink it!" Harry said drily.

Everybody laughed, and Lily told herself that she was beginning to dislike Harry more and more.

She was quite certain that he was the one person aboard who was sceptical about her powers of clairvoyance, and she suspected too that he did not approve of her liaison with the Duke.

Yet she felt that he would not say anything to his friend, and she was shrewd enough to go out of her way to tell the Duke how much she liked all his friends, especially Harry.

She was not yet aware that much of what she talked about when she was with the Duke "went in one ear and out the other," as his Nanny would have said.

He found Lily so lovely that she was part of the beauty of Egypt, the mysterious world of hot, dry sunlight and black shadows, which as they steamed South made him feel as if he were stepping back in time.

He had read many of the innumerable books that he had brought with him, but although nobody aboard noticed it, he had ceased to talk about what he had read.

If Lily had been more astute she would have thought it was significant, but, satisfied as long as he was excited by her beauty, she did not understand that his mind was probing deeper all the time into something new, something fundamental, and in every way the opposite of anything that had interested him before.

He found that the books he read left him with hundreds of questions to which he did not know the answers, and he decided that when he returned to England he would visit the British Museum and find an Egyptologist who could explain many things that puzzled him.

But if everything else was a mystery, one thing he had learnt was that the place of most importance in the days of the most powerful Pharaohs was Thebes. It might be in ruins, but on the opposite bank was Luxor, where they were going.

He had in fact insisted that the yacht, which lay at anchor all night so as not to disturb the sleeping passengers, should leave very early this morning so that he could see Luxor at dawn.

Now as the sun rose a little higher, throwing a rose-coloured light over the cliffs of the Theben hills, the Duke knew he was looking at the burial place of the Pharaohs, known as "The Valley of the Kings."

On the east bank, the pillars of two Temples were silhouetted against the blue of the sky and they had all the magnetic appeal that he was seeking.

He had been told before he left London that at Luxor the Egyptians had been building a luxurious Winter Palace Hotel for tourists from Europe and America, who found the warm climate an attraction in the cold months of the year.

The Duke was not concerned with this, even though he thought it would doubtless amuse his guests.

But as the yacht drew a little nearer he saw a flight of white steps leading from the river up to a Temple whose pillars gleamed brilliantly in the morning sunshine.

He stood looking at it and felt an irresistible desire to enter the Temple, but even as he did so, he knew that more than anything else he wished to go there alone.

He could not explain why he had no desire to be accompanied by anybody, except somehow he felt it would disturb the atmosphere and perhaps himself.

He therefore ordered the yacht to drop anchor on the opposite side of the river.

Although the Captain thought it strange that the

Duke did not wish to be beside the Hotel and Temples
on the other bank, he was too well trained to question
his Master's decision.

When the others appeared later in the morning they
exclaimed with delight at the view opposite them, the
high palm trees shading the banks of the river, and the
feluccas with scimitar-like sacks were everywhere round
them on the Nile.

The Mermaid, being so large, was regarded with
admiration and curiosity by numbers of small, dark-
skinned children splashing about naked in the water, and
along the side of the river under the palm tress there
were the inevitable small donkeys drawing *arabiyas* and
clopping along with sight-seeing visitors.

Because it was very hot, everybody felt relaxed and
lazy and they agreed to the Duke's suggestion that they
should not move until after luncheon, and then if they
wished they could be rowed across the river to the Winter Palace Hotel.

Lily, looking cool and alluring in a white muslin and
lace dress and a large white hat that shaded her beautiful
face, was only too happy to agree to anything which did
not require a great deal of movement.

She disliked getting hot, and if her white skin was
flushed she was always afraid it might clash with her hair.

When finally they were rowed ashore in the ship's
dinghy, she sank down in one of the wicker armchairs on
the verandah of the Winter Palace to be waited on by a
tall Sudanese waiter in a white galabieh with a red sash,
and she had no wish to go any farther.

"What about a bit of exploring?" she heard Jimmy
say to the Duke.

"Tomorrow," the Duke answered. "There is no hurry. I intend to say here for a few days, and if you want a
change of cuisine, we might dine at the Winter Palace
one evening."

"That would be fun!" Amy exclaimed. "I was looking at the guest-list, and although they have not yet arrived, I know the names of quite a number of people who will be staying here later on in the week."

"Then we must certainly ask them on board," the Duke said. "The last thing I would wish you to do is to get bored with your own company or mine."

"How could we do that?" Lily asked softly.

The way she looked at the Duke told him that it would be impossible for her ever to be bored with him.

It was cooler and the shadows were growing deeper and longer when they returned to the yacht.

Only when everybody was seated in the boat which would carry them across the river to where the Duke's staff were waiting to help them on board did he say unexpectedly:

"Go ahead. I will join you later, but I must first stretch my legs."

"Do you want me to come with you?" Harry asked automatically.

"No, Harry. Please look after the party for me."

He walked away quickly before Lily could say anything, and she frowned at the idea of his being alone.

Then she told herself that she had no wish to walk in the dust, and although it was certainly cooler than it had been an hour ago, she would find that any movement, however slow, would be exhausting.

She was well aware that the Duke needed exercise. He had swum every morning from the yacht while they had been moving up the Nile, and although they had teased him and told him he would be attacked by crocodiles, he had continued to dive off the stern.

He also played strenuous Badminton every day with Harry and Jimmy. Occasionally, when Charles could be persuaded to join them, they had a foursome.

"It will do him good," Lily consoled herself, "and he will find me even more alluring when he returns."

As soon as they reached the yacht, she went to her cabin to change into a diaphanous gown that revealed every line of her perfect figure.

Then, instead of joining the others, she went to the Duke's private cabin to lie on the sofa and wait for him.

*   *   *

Alone, the Duke walked briskly along the riverside, knowing that this was what he had been waiting for all day. He was trying to remember what he had read about "The Temple of Luxor," as it was called in the Guide-Books.

He guessed that because he had waited until late in the afternoon, everybody staying in the Hotel would have already visited it, and as he approached the Temple he saw to his relief that there was nobody about.

The massive entrance pylons were flanked outside by six colossal statues of Ramses II in a marvelous state of preservation.

Through these he entered the great pillared Courtyard of Ramses II surrounded by double rows of massive columns, and as they towered above him as he walked between them, the Duke felt not as if he had stepped back into the past but as if he had never left it.

On the far side he could see an impressive colonnade with columns each capped by an "open flower" papyrus capital, which he knew from his reading led into another great open Courtyard.

For some minutes he stood enveloping himself in the atmosphere, almost as if he was listening and using not only his eyes but some inner sense.

Then he moved on silently over the soft sand to

where the shadows seemed almost black in contrast to the white of the pillars.

It was then as he looked from the inside of a small chamber toward the river that he saw the profile of a woman.

For a moment, bemused by his own thoughts, he was not certain whether she was real or engraved on one of the pillars.

He only knew that her straight nose and pointed chin were part of Egypt and what he was seeking.

He stood looking at her, his thoughts refusing to materialise in his mind, at the same time vividly conscious that this was the beauty of the ages.

Then she moved and he realized that she was in fact a real person, although her body had been in the shadows and he had been aware only of her face.

He came nearer, and now, coming as it were back to reality, he saw she that was a young woman, or rather a girl.

Her gown, which had melted into the shadows, was a soft shade of blue, and her hair was neither fair nor dark but a colour which blended into the sun-kissed stone.

As he nearly reached her, as if she had not heard him but was aware of his presence, she turned her face and he found himself looking at a pair of eyes that were startlingly blue.

Instinctively he moved no farther but stood still.

They looked at each other until, as if he were speaking across a chasm instead of the short space which divided them, he said:

"Forgive me if I startled you. I was not aware that there was anybody else here."

For a moment he thought she would not reply. Then she said in a low, musical voice:

"There are few visitors at this time of the evening."

"That was what I had hoped."

He moved nearer and now he saw that she had been looking from between the columns to where in the distance there was an exquisite view across the river toward the Valley of the Kings.

Because he felt he must say something, he remarked, and somehow it was difficult to speak lightly:

"You are too young to be interested in death."

She looked away from him once more towards the distant mystery of the hill-tops which the setting sun was turning to a deeper pink.

"The Egyptian word for 'tomb,' " she said after what seemed to the Duke to be a long pause, "means 'the House of Eternity.' "

"They believed in life after death?"

"Of course," she replied, "and as they had a very clear idea of what it would be like, they took with them everything they thought they would need in the new world to which they were going."

The Duke thought this was what he wanted to learn and had not found in the books he had read, which had merely contained a long list of the Pharaohs and an even longer description of the gods they worshipped.

"Tell me what the Egyptians did believe."

"The survival of the soul was dependent on the preservation of the body," she answered. "If the physical body perished, then so would the spirit."

The Duke thought this explained many things he had not understood before.

Now he knew why the ancient Egyptians had hidden their Pharaohs away in secret Tombs, and why they had taken with them their personal possessions, clothes, jewellery, furniture, their weapons, their chariots, and even food.

"They were a happy people," the girl said quietly.

"People have depicted them as being cruel to the slaves who were building the Pyramids, tyrants to those who served them, and sinful in their private lives . . . but they are wrong."

"How do you know so much about them?" the Duke enquired.

She smiled, and he realised as she did so that she was very lovely, lovelier than anyone he had ever seen before, but also completely different from what he had thought of as his ideal of beauty.

There was a rightness about her in this particular place, as if she belonged as he had thought she did when he had first seen her.

"I live here," she said in answer to his question, and he looked at her in surprise.

"All the year round?"

"Yes. At least since my father came to Luxor."

"And before that?"

"We were moving about the country, sometimes camping in the desert."

He looked at her in astonishment.

She appeared so refined, so fragile with her delicate features and small hands with long thin fingers, that he could not imagine her enduring the heat and hardship of the interminable sands.

"Your father is an Egyptologist?" he asked, as if that must be the explanation.

She smiled again, and he wondered why the question amused her. Then she said:

"That is what he is at heart. But he came to Egypt years ago as a Missionary, and that is his real work."

"A Missionary?"

The Duke could hardly imagine that she was speaking the truth.

He had always thought of Missionaries as tiresome

men who interfered with the established religion of the
natives and generally made a nuisance of themselves in
countries where they were not wanted.

Anyone less like his conception of a Missionary's
daughter than this lovely creature beside him he could
not imagine.

"You speak as if your father is not a very successful
Missionary," he said at length.

She gave a little laugh, and it was a soft, musical
sound that seemed part of the movement of the pine
leaves that had just caught the evening breeze coming
upstream from the river.

"Papa unfortunately fell in love with Egypt," she
said. "It is something people often do, and they find its
history so entrancing that it is like a dream from which
they cannot awaken."

The Duke thought that was exactly what he was
beginning to feel himself.

"I would like to meet your father. I feel he could
tell me many things I want to know but do not understand."

"I wish that were possible, but Papa has been ill for
two weeks with a fever."

She looked at the Duke, then as if she felt she ought
to make some explanation she said:

"I stay with him at night and our servant looks after
him in the day while first I sleep, then I come out here."

"You have had a Doctor to see him?" the Duke asked.

The girl shook her head.

"Papa is a Medical Missionary and I know about
medicines too. We have done everything that is possible,
but Nile fevers are very unpleasant. That is why you
must not come in contact with him."

When she looked at the Duke and thought perhaps
he was nervous that she might be infectious, she explained:

"I think I am immune. I have nursed so many children with fever, and women too, but I have never caught one."

"I cannot imagine you doing such things," the Duke remarked. "When I first saw you I thought you were not real and that your face was carved on the pillar against which you leant, and that you really had lived thousands of years ago."

He spoke lightly, but as she did not answer he added after a silence which seemed to last for a long time:

"Perhaps you did live here in the past!"

As he spoke he thought it was a very strange thing to say and perhaps she would not reply, or would laugh it away. Instead she said:

"I know . . . I did . . . and so . . . did . . . you!"

The Duke stiffened. Then as he looked at her incredulously she said quickly:

"I should not have said that. Forgive me . . . I must return to my . . . father."

She moved away from the pillar and now the Duke saw that she was slender and her waist was very tiny. But she was not short, and she had, he thought, the lithe grace of one of the engraved figures he had noticed when he had first entered the Temple.

She was wearing a gown that was not in the least fashionable, buttoned up to the throat and down the front of the bodice, with a full skirt, plain and unadorned.

Yet, simple though it was, on her it had a grace that was again part of the beauty round them.

"Please do not leave me," the Duke said. "If I cannot see your father, then I want you to answer the questions that trouble me. I promise you I am a very serious student of the land that has drawn me irrepressibly for no reason I can understand."

Because he so desperately wanted her to stay, the Duke exerted all the charm that had never failed him in the past.

He knew as she stood looking at him indecisively that she was trying to make up her mind as to what she should do.

"Tell me about the Temple," he begged.

He felt as he spoke that what was worrying her was that inadvertently she had said something too personal, and now, like a child who has done something wrong, she wanted to run away and forget it.

"How much do you . . . know about it . . . already?" she asked.

He thought from her tone that she was attempting to sound matter-of-fact and speak as if it were of little importance.

"I must confess an abysmal ignorance," the Duke replied.

She gave a little laugh. Then as she walked back into the Courtyard he said:

"I think perhaps we should introduce ourselves. I am the Duke of Darleston, and I arrived only this morning in the yacht which you can see moored on the other side of the river."

"I noticed it."

As if he could read her thoughts, he knew she was comparing it somewhat unfavourably with the barges that had been used by the Pharaohs, or perhaps the one with the silken, scented sails which had carried Cleopatra down the Nile to Mark Antony.

He also felt that a Duke was hardly in the same category as a Pharaoh.

"Now tell me your name," he said.

"Irisa," she replied, and he smiled.

"It suits you. And your other name?"

He thought she hesitated for just a moment before she said:

"Garron."

As if she had no wish for him to comment, she pointed out to him some of the details of the Great Court.

The Duke was interested, but he had a feeling that she was talking almost like a Guide rather than as she had spoken before, as her own person.

"They have been doing some excavations here," she said, "and there is a great deal more to do. As you see, the Temple has, over the centuries, been built on by other religions."

As she spoke she pointed, and the Duke saw a small Mosque built onto the wall of the Courtyard from the outside and perched high above the original ground level.

A strange contrast," he said, "and yet I believe that all religions are good for the people who believe in them."

"Of course they are!" Irisa replied. "So it is ridiculous for outsiders to try to force another religion on people who have their own."

"If your father feels the same way, I can understand why he has given up being a Missionary to concentrate on Ancient Egypt," the Duke commented.

"I did not say he had done so," Irisa said quickly.

"Then perhaps I read your thoughts."

"It is something you . . . must not . . . do!"

"Why not?"

"Because thoughts are a very intimate part of oneself and to read them would be an intrusion."

"I do not think I have ever before been able to do so," the Duke replied, "but when you were speaking just now I was aware of a great deal you did not say, just as I think you feel the same about me."

As he spoke he was astonished to hear the words that seemed to have come involuntarily to his lips and the voice that spoke them was his own.

"Why should you . . . say that?"

"Perhaps you have cast a spell over me," he answered, "or perhaps it is the Temple itself. I only know that I feel as if I have stepped through the veil that parts one world from the other, and now this is just as real to me as the world I have left."

She turned quickly to face him, and now as the setting sun turned everything to a deep gold, her hair seemed to glow as it had not done before and her eyes were vividly blue.

"You frighten me," she whispered. "I thought when I first saw you I was dreaming and when we spoke to each other I was still asleep. Now I am awake and I want you to go . . . away and . . . forget you have . . . met me."

"Why should I do that?" the Duke asked. "I want to talk to you. If you believe in fate, as I know you do, then you believe it was not by chance that I came here tonight alone to the Temple and that you were here waiting for me."

"I was not . . . waiting . . ." she began.

Then her voice died away and she made a helpless gesture, as if it was impossible to try to refute what he had said.

"Let us accept," he urged, "that the gods, or whoever is watching over our destiny, have brought us together for a purpose, and that, as far as I am concerned, is to learn what is hidden from those who write very dull books about Egypt and who think that the past has no bearing on the future."

He realised as he spoke that his words had moved her, and she clasped her hands together as she said:

"I understand, because . . . that is what I . . . too think. There is so much here we could learn if we are . . . prepared to listen . . . so much that would help the . . . people of this nation and . . . others."

"Then begin by teaching me what I should know,

and perhaps I shall have the power to bring it to the notice of people who matter."

"Can you do . . . that?"

She asked the question simply, as a child might have done.

"I hope so," the Duke answered, "but first, as you can understand, I have to be utterly and completely convinced that what I am saying is true."

"Yes, of course," she replied, "but perhaps I am not the right person to . . . teach you. If only Papa was here tonight it would be . . . different."

"I think we should take one step at a time," the Duke said. "The first step for me is to listen to a goddess called Irisa."

She smiled as if she understood that he was comparing her to the great goddess Isis who was depicted on so many of the columns.

She led him beyond the Mosque to where there were eleven red granite statues of Pharaohs and among them a diminutive replica of Queen Nefretiri.

She did not speak, she only stood still, and the Duke looked at the statue as she intended him to do.

The Queen was very beautiful with her luxuriant, thick plaits of hair flowing from her head to cover her breasts. Her lovely face showed no lines of worry and her mouth curved in the suspicion of a smile.

She looked happy, and at the same time she was demure and dignified as befitted a Queen.

"Is this who you were?" the Duke asked softly.

Irisa shook her head.

"No."

"Then who?"

"I do not wish to . . . speak of it . . . now."

"But you will do so another time?"

"P-perhaps."

She hesitated over the word, and he had a feeling that she did not want to tell him because she was shy, but he was afraid to tell her so.

They moved on to look at Temple reliefs which showed the splendour of the processions which had taken place between the Temple of Luxor and that of Karnak.

"I want to see Karnak tomorrow," the Duke said.

He looked at her as he spoke, and she knew he was asking her to show him the Great Temple of Arnon, on which every guide-book expended pages and pages of description.

"I will show it to you," she said after a moment's pause, "but it is not as beautiful as this Temple, and there is not the same atmosphere."

"I will be able to tell you what I feel after I have seen it."

He knew as he spoke that he must make quite certain she did not disappear and he could not find her again.

He realised the shadows were lengthening and growing darker and when the sun sank they would be in darkness, for night would come swiftly.

"I will take you back to where you live," he said.

"There is no . . . need."

"It is something I wish to do. Is it really wise for you to wander about here alone?"

"I will come to no harm," she replied. "The people know me and they respect Papa."

"Even when he tries to convert them?"

"I am afraid he does not try very hard, not nowadays."

"Then what does he do?"

The Duke thought she was not going to answer the question, but after a moment she said:

"Ever since we came here he has been interested in the excavations and the discoveries made in the Tombs."

"I can understand that."

"He believes there is a great deal more than has not been discovered, and thieves are still at work, finding treasures which they sell to the tourists, especially the Americans."

"And yet, I understand that quite a number of investigators have said there is nothing more to be found."

Irisa smiled.

"Papa does not believe that . . . nor do I."

"Why not?"

"Because we know from documents only recently translated that there are a great number of Pharaohs buried secretly in Tombs deep down in the cliffs, which even the robbers have not found."

"But they will eventually," the Duke said.

"So Papa hopes."

"And you?"

"I am quite happy to think back into the past and imagine what those sleeping Kings or Queens were like when they were alive."

"You say they were happy?"

"A very happy people."

"And you are happy too?"

She smiled in answer, and he thought that although it reminded him of the smile on the lips of Queen Nefretiri, it was far lovelier.

"Yes, you are happy!" he said positively.

It was only much later that he thought how strange it was that he should find a Missionary's daughter, obviously poor, living in a strange land, apparently with no friends and her only companion her father, happy in a way which no other woman of his acquaintance ever appeared to be.

Now Irisa was leading the way out to the back of the Temple where there were palm trees in a sandy wasteland.

There were also a few mud huts and the inevitable small, naked children playing games round them.

Then there was a clump of tall palm trees and shrubs vivid with blossom and a house.

Long and low, it was made of wood with a verandah reached by a flight of steps running across the front of it.

Above the verandah there was a small cross and behind it, somewhat incongruously, a ragged Union Jack.

"So this is where you live!" the Duke said.

"I cannot invite you in," Irisa said as they stopped near the shrubs. "I would not wish you to catch Nile fever."

"I am grateful that you are thinking of me," the Duke answered.

He spoke automatically, but as he did so he was aware that it was actually what she was doing.

She put out her hand and he took it in his.

For the first time since their meeting he realised that it was unconventional and certainly unusual for her not to be wearing a hat.

Instead, her hair was drawn back into a large coil at the back of her neck and held in place by hair-pins and a small bow of blue ribbon.

It somehow looked a little frivolous compared to the severity with which she was otherwise dressed.

"I do not know how grateful I am," the Duke said, "for having met you and for what you have taught me so far."

He spoke with an intensity that surprised himself, and as Irisa's eye-lashes flickered over her blue eyes he realised that he had made her shy.

"I will wait for you tomorrow at the same place."

For a moment she did not answer, and he said urgently:

"Please do not fail me!"

"I . . . I might not be . . . able to come."

"That is a prevarication and untrue," he said. "You told me you sleep in the daytime, so shall I say I will meet you at the Temple where we met this evening at the same time? Or perhaps just a little earlier, as we have to go to Karnak."

"I will . . . try."

She would have moved away from him, but he held on to her hand.

"I want your promise—a promise you will not break. By whichever god the Egyptians swear at such a moment at this."

There was a faint smile on Irisa's lips as she replied after a moment's thought:

"Thoth is the God of Wisdom."

"And therefore of the truth," the Duke added. "So swear to me by Thoth that you will come to me tomorrow night and not leave me waiting and wondering if I have been dreaming, and fearing that when I come here in search of you the house will have disappeared."

As he spoke he felt he was being a little unsportsmanlike in threatening her, and as if she understood exactly what he was doing she said:

"It is too . . . trivial a matter with which to . . . worry the gods. I will come if my father is well enough. If he is not, I will send a messenger to . . . tell you that I am . . . detained."

"Thank you," the Duke replied.

Her eyes met his, then as if she suddenly realised for the first time who he was and was conscious of his importance, she dropped him a small curtsey.

"Good-night, Your Grace," she said, and walked through the gap in the shrubs toward the wooden house.

The Duke waited and thought that when she reached the steps and climbed onto the wooden verandah she would turn and look back.

He had never known a woman who did not look

back when she had left him, and he waited, ready to smile and wave.

Irisa, however, walked straight across the verandah and in through the half-open door.

She left the Duke with an apprehensive feeling that perhaps what the gods had given, the gods would take away and he would never see her again.

Chapter Five

The Duke awoke early and lay planning his day as he had started to do last night.

When he had got back to the yacht he had found it difficult to adjust himself to the chatter and laughter of his guests.

They were sitting on deck, drinking champagne, and as he saw at once that Lily was not with them, he knew where she would be.

He was aware that he had no wish at the moment either to talk to her or touch her. So he waited until it was time to dress for dinner, then deliberately went straight to his bed-cabin, where his valet was waiting and had prepared a bath for him.

He knew that Lily would hear him talking to the man, if she was still in the cabin next door, and would understand that he was not joining her as she had expected.

If she had waited all that time, Lily was too clever to

look reproachful when the Duke joined them all before dinner.

Instead, she had arrayed herself in one of her most becoming evening-gowns. It was white, like all of her clothes, but it was very elaborate and she wore every jewel she possessed so that she glittered like the stars that were coming out overhead.

She planned that she would ask the Duke to take her on deck while the others played Bridge.

But, to her surprise, after dinner was over he sat down at the card-table and challenged Lord Southwold to a game in which they had very large side-bets which did not affect the other players.

Despite everything she tried to do, Lily could not capture the Duke's attention. So instead she flirted with James Bushly, making it appear obvious that she found him attractive, and hoped the Duke would be jealous.

When finally they retired to bed, Lily was sure the Duke would come to her as he had done every night since they had reached the Mediterranean. But as the hours went by she knew that, for some reason she could not ascertain, she had for tonight, at any rate, lost his interest.

The Duke hardly gave a thought to the fact that Lily was waiting for him.

All the time he played Bridge he was longing to be alone so that he could think over the strange and unusual things that had happened at the Temple of Luxor and the girl who had opened the windows of his mind to new horizons which he had not known existed.

It was not only what she had said, it was what she was, or perhaps she had put a spell on him.

He had read somewhere, or else he had known it instinctively, that the Egyptians saw magic in everything round them, and because he was a very intelligent man, he reasoned to himself that they found the life-force,

which was for them the Divine Spirit, in every creature
and especially in animals.

Why else, he asked, would animals in human form
play such a prominent role in their system of worship?

He had seen the gods with animal-heads on the
columns in the Temple and had read in one of the books
he had studied that the Sky-god Horus had the head of a
falcon, the Goddess of War the head of a lioness, the God
of the Cataracks that of a ram, and the Moon-god that of
an ibis.

He lay thinking, trying to understand, and he thought,
although he was certain it must be his imagination, that
Irisa was also thinking of him.

'She will tell me more tomorrow evening,' he told
himself, and knew the idea was exciting in a way that was
different from any excitement he had felt in the past.

He had told his valet before dinner to arrange for
him to have breakfast early alone in his cabin, and to
order two horses, one with a Guide, to be waiting beside
the yacht.

He wanted to explore and he had no intention of
riding one of the small donkeys that were provided for
tourists.

It was still very early and he was sure everybody
else was asleep in their cabins when he walked on deck
into the already brilliant sunshine and saw the Theban
hills glowing pink from its rays.

The horses waiting for him were the small-boned,
fidgety little animals which were far stronger than they
looked, and they appeared not to mind the overwhelming
heat as a European horse would have done.

The Guide was a tall, dark-skinned man with hand-
some features, wearing the usual white galabieh with a
black robe over it and a turban.

Having greeted the Duke respectfully, he led off in
the direction of the hills.

The horses were fresh and at first they moved quickly, then the Duke deliberately drew in his mount because he wished to look round him.

He also felt, as he had yesterday, the spell of the place enveloping him, and as he saw ahead the mysteries of the Valley of the Kings, he remembered that Irisa had said that the Tombs were "Houses of Eternity."

Today the Duke had no wish to visit the few empty Tombs that had already been excavated but wished merely to look at the countryside and to sense the atmosphere.

The sun rose higher and it was very hot, but he was too intent to think of what he was feeling physically while he concentrated on what he felt in his mind.

He had already told his valet to inform the Guide that he had no wish to talk unless he asked questions, and accordingly they rode in silence until, as the man had pointed in the direction he wished to go, the Duke saw on the ground in front of him a huge, dark granite head.

He realised it was a head from the colossus of a Pharaoh which must once have adorned a Temple.

He was not interested in who had been carved in such gigantic proportions. But the Guide said quietly:

"Ramses II said: 'I did good to the gods as well as to men and took possession of nothing belonging to other people.'"

The Duke found the head lying by itself on the ground somehow moving, as if it typified the end of a Dynasty which in its time had played a great part in the history of the world but was now forgotten.

He rode on to look at an amazingly well-preserved Temple which the Guide told him had been built for Queen Hatshepsut.

The man was obviously anxious for the Duke to dismount and inspect the Temple, and he could see that on the walls sheltered by a many-pillared portico there were many inscriptions coloured flame and turquoise and depicting gods and goddesses with their strange animal-heads.

Again, he was not interested in detail. He only wanted to look, think, and above all—to feel.

*   *   *

When Lily learnt that the Duke had left the yacht very early, she was annoyed.

She had been so certain that he found her irresistible, and the ardour of his love-making had lulled her into a false sense of security.

Now she was alarmed.

Then she was sure that such fears were needless.

He had gone riding only with a Guide, and if he found any women in the Valley of the Kings they would either be mummies or engraved on the ruined Temples and were not likely to constitute any danger to their relationship.

She had always heard that The Dasher was unpredictable, and she supposed that after being cooped up in the yacht for so long he wanted to be free and alone.

She told herself that she would be very stupid if she let him think that she was clinging to him or shackling him in any way.

The stories of how he had avoided matrimony for so long had lost nothing in the telling, and the gossips had described in detail the failure of the many women who had tried to capture him.

"I will not fail!" Lily swore.

She thought of the fire in the Duke's eyes when he kissed her, his excitement when he touched her, and his passion, which exceeded anything she had ever known before.

He loved her! She knew he loved her!

But as the Duke was not there, she contented herself with flirting with Lord Southwold, who was only too willing to substitute for his host.

On any other occasion Lily thought such a very rich man would have been useful to her, and she was quite certain that Lord Southwold, given the opportunity, would be an exceedingly generous lover.

But she had come on the trip determined to marry the most elusive and fascinating bachelor in England, and she was not prepared to be side-tracked into doing anything which might conceivably annoy him.

However, because he was not there, she talked to Lord Southwold about his financial interests and beguiled him with her prophecies of huge successes, enormous profits, and even greater developments in the future.

At the same time, while painting such a glowing picture, she added warnings of the necessity for caution, which made him more certain than he had been already that she could really see into the future.

After luncheon they went ashore as they had done the day before, to walk leisurely in the beautiful garden of the Winter Palace Hotel and then to sit sipping deliciously cool drinks on the verandah.

Two people whom the Southwolds knew had just arrived from England, and as they were socially distinguished and obviously very wealthy, Lily was delighted to make their acquaintance.

Only as the afternoon wore on did she say almost involuntarily to Harry:

"What can have happened to His Grace? I do hope he has not met with an accident or fallen amongst thieves!"

"I am sure The Dasher can look after himself."

"I hope so," Lily said. "At the same time, I cannot help feeling there is a chance of danger."

She spoke in the same mysterious voice that she

used when speaking to Lord Southwold, then realised
that Harry's eyes were mocking as he answered:

"If you want my opinion, the only danger at the
moment is that our host will find his voyage of discovery
disappointing and want to return home."

Lily gave a little cry.

"Oh, I hope not!" she said. "It is so lovely here that
I have no desire to move anywhere else."

"Then it is up to you," Harry remarked.

She knew he was taunting her, and she hated him.
Nevertheless, she gave him one of her beguiling smiles
as she said:

"I think we must all be very, very nice to our dashing Duke when he comes back from the wilds."

However, she looked, even if she did not sound it,
worried by his absence, and she thought as she turned to
speak to somebody else that Harry was pleased at her
frustration.

*   *   *

The Duke had in fact made his return to the yacht
when he knew his party would have crossed the Nile. He
was hot and hungry, but at the same time he had enjoyed
every moment of his ride and the exploration of the
Theban hills.

He thought as he looked at them that they had a
glory and at the same time a glamour he had never found
anywhere else.

Barren and bare as the rocks were, he was sure that
Irisa would tell him that they breathed the mystery of
eternal life.

He felt too that they stimulated his mind and gave
him an impetus to seek and go on seeking until he found
the answer that was waiting for him.

He bathed, changed his clothes, had an excellent luncheon which his Chef had started to prepare as soon as he appeared, then was ready to cross the river to the steps which led directly down from the Temple of Luxor to the water.

He was early and he expected to have to wait for some time before Irisa appeared, but she was there exactly where she had been the day before.

She was looking out in the same way, her little straight nose and softly curved chin silhouetted against the same pillar.

He stood watching her for some moments before she was aware of him, then as a faint smile touched her lips he moved towards her and she turned her head.

"You are there!" he said in his deep voice. "All night I have been half-afraid that you were a dream and I would never find you again."

"I promised to take you to Karnak, and I always try to keep my promises."

She walked away as she spoke, and a moment later he understood that she was taking him to Karnak by boat.

He felt that the reason for it was not because it was an easier way of approach but because he would approach the Temple in the manner intended by those who had built it.

As they stood waiting on the white steps of the Temple for the felucca to pick them up, the Duke felt that he was embarking on a voyage to another land.

Everything he had read about Karnak had bewildered him because it was difficult to understand what the author was trying to say, and yet now as they journeyed slowly towards the greatest Temple in Egypt, the Duke began to realise its significance.

He had read that Karnak covered four hundred acres by the riverside, and he knew that brilliant paintings had adorned its walls and steles of lapis-lazuli were set on both sides of the foremost pylon, of which there were ten in all.

Vast quantities of malachite, silver, and gold covered the facade, while over all, glowing with magic, was the colossus of the Pharaoh, hewn from gritstone, soaring sixty-seven feet into the air.

He was not certain afterwards whether Irisa had said it aloud or he had merely read her mind.

It had taken the Egyptians eight hundred years to build it, and now the columns were bare of colour. But the moment they entered the Temple with its gigantic columns seventy feet in height, the Duke was conscious that the whole effect was of an overwhelming, mind-crushing power.

The atmosphere was so different from that of the Temple of Luxor that at first it was hard to collect his thoughts.

Then as he walked in silence, with Irisa moving so lightly beside him that her feet seemed to make hardly any impression in the sand, he knew that here the gods had ruled by fear and their majesty had no humanity.

Many of the reliefs on the columns were strikingly beautiful, and he would have stopped to look at them if Irisa had not seemed to wish him to move on.

He was content to follow her, feeling that she had some reason for where she was taking him.

They passed an enormous relief depicting conquests and sacrifices, then she paused and the Duke could see ahead the Sacred Lake, although she evidently did not intend to go there at the moment.

She was looking at him, he thought, in a strange manner, almost as if she was convincing herself that what she was doing was right, and there was also something which made the Duke feel as if she was testing him.

They had hardly spoken more than a few words

since they had met, and yet words had been unnecessary, and he knew that they communicated with each other in their thoughts and he was content just to be with her.

Now as the huge columns rising overpoweringly above them made them seem tiny and insignificant, the Duke had an irresistible impulse to cry out that he was alive when the Temple itself was dead.

And yet he knew it was not true. So much that was life still remained within it.

As the thought came to him, he knew that in some strange, mysterious manner he could not explain, it was what Irisa wanted him to feel.

She gave him a little smile and put out her hand, and when he took it in his he felt her fingers tremble as if they spoke instead of her lips.

"Come," she said very softly. "I have . . . something to show . . . you."

Drawing him by the hand, she walked towards the end of what appeared to the Duke to be a small Temple.

Ahead he could see some very old and dilapidated bronze gates. One of them was open and Irisa drew him through it and with her free hand closed it behind them.

In front of them was a low chamber, and as they walked into it the sunlight vanished, and at first the Duke could see nothing and was conscious only of the damp, chilly darkness.

Irisa was standing quite still and he held on to her hand almost as if he was afraid he might lose her.

Then as his eyes grew accustomed to the darkness, he was aware that there was light filtering through a tiny hole in the ceiling, and he saw that standing quite close to them there was a female figure.

It was the body of a young woman with rounded hips and firm breasts, but the face was that of a lioness.

It was so unexpected, so different from the huge

monstrous columns outside with the blazing sunshine gilding everything with a brilliant light, that the Duke could only look at what he remembered now was the Goddess of War.

Then in an unexpected manner the goddess vanished and he saw clearly a vision in the darkness.

He could never determine afterwards whether the scene was in his mind or if it was actually portrayed in the cell-like sanctuary.

He was now a warrior wearing armour and in command of a number of men who were marching beside him.

He knew they had just arrived by river and had disembarked from a ship in which they had travelled a great distance. They were tired after such a long voyage, but at the same time they were elated because they had reached their destination.

He had been given orders to escort and protect someone who was carried on a litter on the shoulders of six strong men. The Duke looked up and saw that the Princess from the land whence they had come was Irisa!

He saw her face framed with jewels, and he knew she was decked in her finest robes because she had come to Egypt as a bride for the Pharaoh.

As they moved on, the Duke knew that he loved with every breath he drew the woman who had been entrusted to his charge, and whom he had brought as the bride of another man.

He was aware that as soon as he had given her into the hands of the Egyptians, he would return to his own country and never see her again. Yet, he would leave his heart with her.

It was an agony as they neared the great Palace of the Pharaoh to know that while he loved the Princess and she also loved him, there was nothing either of them could do about it.

The Duke was not even sure if they had told each other of what they felt, but words were unnecessary.

Their love linked them together as closely as if they were one person, and it was a love which they had known in the past and would never die.

He was aware in his soldier's mind that the Pharaohs usually took as their Great Chief Wife their sisters or even occasionally their own daughters.

In pre-Dynastic times, property and possessions were transferred through the female line—by matrilineal rather than patrilineal descent.

So, to secure his title beyond the faintest shadow of doubt, the Pharaoh married every woman who could possibly lay claim to the throne.

In addition to his principal and much venerated Queen, he would also possess what might be called "Political Wives"—foreign Princesses who were sent by their fathers to marry the King of Egypt in order to cement a diplomatic alliance.

There might also be "wives" who were bought and introduced into the Royal *harim*, but the children of the Great Chief Wife and the Political Wives were recognised as Princes or Princesses and they were also endowed with some of the great might and majesty and god-like qualities of the Pharaoh himself.

All this flashed through the mind of the Duke as he escorted the Princess on her carved and gilded litter.

Then as he looked up and her blue eyes met his, they both cried out at the cruelty of the separation ahead.

Yet there was nothing they could do but say a silent "good-bye" and try to believe that their love would endure through the rest of their lives or perhaps, by some strange power they did not understand, surmount death and the grave.

Ahead of them the Duke could see the soldiers of

the Pharaoh and his servants coming out to greet the
new bride. There were women with flowers and children carrying rose-petals to sprinkle on her path.

Once again he looked up into the blue eyes search-
ing his face.

"Good-bye, my love," he said in his heart.

Then there was darkness.

The vision had gone and there was just a light on the
lion-headed goddess.

*   *   *

A long time later, or it may have been only a few
minutes, the Duke found himself sitting at the side of
the Sacred Lake.

Irisa was beside him and as he looked down at the
still water where the Priests had reverently lowered the
Royal cedar barge containing the body of a dead Pharaoh, he wondered whether he had suddenly become
insane or had taken a drug which had induced strange
visions.

Never in his life had he ever not been in complete
control of his mind and his body, and he had believed
that it was impossible for anyone to hypnotise him.

Now he wondered whether that was what Irisa had
done. Then he knew that was not true.

The water touched by the sun was dazzling, and in a
voice which did not sound like his own the Duke asked:

"Did you see what I saw?"

There was a little pause before Irisa replied:

"I have . . . seen it in the . . . past."

"You saw how we parted, I suppose in a—previous
life?"

"Yes, but there may have been others."

"Other lives?"

"Perhaps . . . I do not . . . know. In Egypt you will only . . . see the ones that happened . . . here."

"To me it is unacceptable, but you believe it to be true."

The Duke felt as if he forced the question from her and after a moment she said:

"I know you suspect me of trickery in some way, but it would be impossible."

"Where did you take me?"

"To the sanctuary of the Goddess Sekhmet. It is the only sanctuary in the whole of Karnak which still houses the image of a Deity."

"And you found it yourself? Or does everybody know about it?"

"The Guides never take visitors there. They are afraid. But Papa found it soon after we first came to Luxor, and I think it was there that he knew he had been brought here for a purpose."

"What purpose?"

"I would like him to tell you that himself, when he is well enough."

The Duke was silent for a moment. Then he said:

"I am still feeling greatly disturbed by what I have seen, and you can understand that I am trying to find an explanation."

Irisa laughed and it seemed somehow as if the sound rippled across the Sacred Lake and took away some of the overwhelming menace of the great Temple behind them.

"Why are you laughing?" the Duke asked.

"Because you are being so English! You are just like Papa when he first came here and suspected everybody of being a charlatan! 'There must be a reasonable explanation for this!' he would say to me, until he found it was entirely reasonable that we had lived before."

She waited for the Duke to argue with her, and when he did not do so, she went on:

"Just as the Nile never dries up, so life continues, season after season, year after year, century after century."

The Duke was suddenly aware that the sun was deepening red on the horizon and he rose to his feet.

"I must take you home," he said. "Sensible and unimaginative as I am trying to prove myself to be, I do not wish to be lost in Karnak in the darkness."

"You would not be harmed," Irisa said, "but I agree, it would be frightening."

They walked back through the rows of pillars which seemed to the Duke to have been placed too close to each other, perhaps in order to proclaim deliberately a power against which there was no defence.

They passed through the Forecourt of Amum and the Temples of various Pharaohs with heraldic pillars until at last they came to the stone steps leading down to the river.

By now the sun was only a streak of burning crimson on the horizon, and by the time they reached the Temple of Luxor the river had turned from gold to purple.

The Temple seemed to welcome them and once again the Duke took Irisa's hand as they moved past the beautiful columns and out on the other side to the waste-land with its mud huts.

There was still enough light to lead them to the wooden house protected by the high palm trees, and when they reached the shrubs Irisa halted.

"We will meet again tomorrow?" the Duke asked.

"Perhaps I have . . . shown you all . . . you wish to . . . see?"

"You know without my saying it that I must see you, and I have only touched the fringe of what I want to know and hear."

"After what has . . . happened today, you may be disappointed with . . . everything else."

"That is for me to judge," he replied. "All I want to make certain of is that I shall find you in the same place at the same time. You will promise to come?"

She hesitated, and he was suddenly afraid.

"Please, Irisa, you know as well as I do that I cannot lose you, and you cannot leave me gasping at the incredibility of what you have made me see and feel. You must help me to understand."

"I do not think you really need my help."

"I promise you I want it more than I have ever wanted anything before. I am like a drowning man, Irisa, and you have to save me!"

She smiled as if there was something ridiculous in his portraying himself as being so helpless. Then looking up at him she said:

"I was afraid at first that I might be . . . mistaken, but now I am glad, so very glad, that my instinct was right and you are . . . who I thought you . . . would be."

"What you are saying is that you recognised me when we first met?"

She nodded her head.

"I suppose really," the Duke said reflectively after a moment, "that I recognised you when I thought your face was carved on the pillar against which you were standing. It seemed familiar, but it is something which if spoken out loud would seem absurd."

"Of course," she said, "as I have already told you, it is difficult when you first come here to adjust yourself. But in time, as something . . . happens every day, it grows easier."

"That is what you have to convince me."

He made an impatient little sound.

"I do not want you to leave now, I want to go on talking to you. It is more frustrating than I can possibly explain to have to wait until tomorrow afternoon before I can see you again, but I realise you have to sleep if you watch over your father all night."

It was obvious that he was reasoning it out for himself. Then he said:

"I have had no chance to tell you, but today I rode to the Valley of the Kings."

"Yes, I know."

He raised his eye-brows.

"How do you know?"

She smiled.

"Everybody knows everything in this small place. Ali, one of our servants who works in the gardens, told me you had hired horses, and I thought it very wise of you to do so, rather than go alone."

"I might have gone completely alone," the Duke said, "if I had not been afraid of losing my way, but I told my Guide not to chatter."

"You were sensible in that at any rate. And what did you do when you reached the Burial Ground of the Pharaohs?"

"I only stayed a little while," the Duke said, "as I wanted to go again with you."

"I think . . . perhaps it would be . . . impossible."

"Why?"

She obviously did not wish to explain. Instead she said:

"Perhaps we can talk about it . . . another time."

"And you will come tomorrow?"

She was just about to answer when there was a sudden cry that seemed to echo into the night.

They both turned and saw standing on the verandah a man in white.

He looked about him wildly across the flowers and shrubs, then he saw Irisa and cried:

"Missy, come quick! Come!"

It seemed to the Duke as if Irisa flew from his side.
She sped towards the steps leading up to the verandah
and climbed them and vanished into the house almost
before he could catch his breath.

It was then, slowly and deliberately, that he followed
her.

The wooden steps creaked beneath his feet and he
walked across the verandah and entered through the
open door.

He saw by the faint light coming from another room
that he had entered what was obviously a Sitting-Room
with windows on both sides of it.

It was already too dark to have an impression of
anything but the outlines of furniture, and he walked
towards a light and found himself in the doorway of a
small square bedroom on the other side of the house.

Lying on a wooden bed covered only with a white
sheet was a man, and kneeling beside him was Irisa.

One glance at the man on the bed told the Duke
that he was dead.

He stood in the doorway, not certain what he should
do, aware that Irisa's father was, as he might have expected,
an exceedingly good-looking man.

His features were clear-cut and very English. The
hair at the sides of his head was streaked with grey, and
he was extremely thin.

But the Duke was certain that his high forehed de-
noted intelligence, and he regretted that now it was too
late for him to speak to the man who could have told him
so much.

There was still Irisa, and he saw that while she was
kneeling beside her father, the fingers of one hand were
on his pulse, the other hand was on his heart, and she
was calm and controlled in a manner that he admired.

Then, as if she recognised that her father was dead,

she crossed his hands on his chest and, rising to her feet, drew the sheet very gently over him.

She spoke in Arabic to the servant waiting at the end of the bed. He nodded and the Duke stood aside to allow him to pass through the door, cross the Sitting-Room, and go out of the house.

He waited until Irisa looked at him. Then he said:

"I am sorry. I wished so much to meet your father."

"And I wanted . . . him to know . . . you."

She stood looking down at the body that lay on the bed, then she lifted one of the candles from the table and carried it into the Sitting-Room.

It was a thick white candle in a wooden holder and it illuminated the room, which the Duke could now see was furnished poorly but in good taste.

He liked the simple wicker chairs which were unpretentious but practical in a land where it was always hot.

Then he saw that on the shelves and tables round the room there were pieces of pottery, carvings, and figurines which he was sure had come from the Tombs.

As if he had asked the question, Irisa said:

"They were presents to Papa from those he treated, and, although it seems somewhat . . . reprehensible, they stole what they did not have to give."

"I am sure some of these things are very valuable."

"I would not wish to . . . sell them," Irisa replied, "but I am afraid I shall . . . have to."

As she spoke she sat down in one of the wicker chairs and the Duke thought she had done so because she found she had not the strength to go on standing.

"Now that your father is dead," he said gently, "what are you going to do? You cannot stay here alone."

She made a little sound that was half a sigh and half a sob.

"I suppose not . . . but I would . . . like to . . . stay."

"Unless you have friends who will look after you, you must realise that is impossible."

There was silence and he realised that she was striving desperately to find some way of keeping the house which was, to her, home.

"To whom does it belong?" the Duke asked, and she was aware that he had followed her thoughts.

"The Missionary Society," she answered, "and I suppose now when they learn of Papa's death they will send another man to take his place."

"He will be eager for converts," the Duke remarked, "until the magic of Egypt captivates him as it captivated your father."

He thought he brought a faint smile to her lips. Then she said:

"Perhaps he . . . will need an . . . assistant."

The Duke shook his head.

"He will more likely have a wife and half-a-dozen children!"

"Then . . . I must . . . go . . . home."

He could barely hear the words, and yet she had said them.

"Do you mean to England?"

She nodded as if it was difficult to speak, and after a moment he asked:

"You have relatives there who will look after you?"

"I suppose I must go to my grandfather, but I have not . . . seen him since I was . . . a baby."

"It is not likely he would refuse to have you, considering you are alone."

As he spoke, the Duke thought that Irisa's grandfather or any other relative who might be alive would be surprised at her beauty and also at her intelligence.

How could it be possible that anybody could behave so bravely in such circumstances?

He knew without her telling him that her father had meant everything in her life, and that her security and safety was gone. She was alone in a strange land where it would be impossible for her to look after herself.

It was one thing, the Duke thought, to be the daughter of a Missionary and be protected by the very sanctity of her father's calling, but another to be a very lovely young girl who had barely reached womanhood and must try to cope alone and unprotected.

He felt himself shudder at the thought of what might happen to her, and after a moment he said:

"As you have to return to England, I will take you there."

He knew as she looked at him in a rather startled fashion that the idea had never crossed her mind, and he thought that no other woman, having met him, would have been prepared to let him pass out of her life without even a backwards glance.

"But . . . I cannot . . . ask you to do . . . that," she said.

"Why not?" the Duke enquired. "There is plenty of room in my yacht, and I am quite prepared to wait until you have packed and tidied things up, and of course buried your father."

Irisa clasped her hands together, and after a moment she said:

"I feel I would be . . . imposing myself upon you, and I am quite certain your . . . friends will not . . . want me . . . but for the moment . . . it is difficult to think of what else I . . . can do."

"Then I suggest that you leave everything to me," the Duke said quietly.

Afterwards he realised that it was his attitude of authority that made everything easy for Irisa.

She had sent the servant to fetch embalmers, and while they were working, the copper-maker and grave-diggers had come from one of the scattered mud huts to await instructions.

He learnt that there was at the moment no Christian Priest in luxor and it had been arranged that the Services for those who desired them should be conducted by Irisa's father, who had been ordained before he became a Missionary.

There was, however, a small Cemetery which the Reverend Patrick Garron had himself set aside for the burial of the few Christians who followed his creed.

There had been very few, and the Duke suspected that they had paid him lip-service because they liked him as a man rather than because he had lured them away from the gods they had worshipped since they were born.

As was usual in the East, the Duke arranged for the burial to take place early the next morning, and he paid the grave-diggers to work by moonlight.

Then he went in search of Irisa and found that the embalmers had finished their work and she was kneeling beside her father's bed, and he thought she was praying. When he appeared in the doorway, she rose to her feet.

He took her hand and stood looking down at her father, who appeared serene and at peace.

He was dressed in a clean white skirt, with his hands crossed on his chest, and Irisa had placed between his fingers a lotus-flower that was just coming into bud.

As the Duke looked at it, as if once again she read his thoughts she said:

"The emblem of . . . love and . . . eternal life. Papa is not . . . dead, and one day we shall . . . meet again."

Her voice broke a little but she did not cry, and the Duke tightened his fingers on her hand.

"I know he would want you to think like that."

"Of course," she answered. "He always believed that death was quite unimportant . . . just the discarding of a body that is worn out and is no longer of any use."

She spoke in her soft voice that seemed almost like music.

Then the Duke drew her from the bedroom and back into the Sitting-Room.

"Will you come to the yacht with me now," he asked, "or do you want to stay here tonight?"

It was something he would never have suggested to any other woman, but he knew already, without even asking the question, that Irisa would not wish to leave her father.

"I will . . . stay here," she said, "and of course . . . if tomorrow you change you mind . . . and do not . . . want me . . . I will . . . understand."

"There is no question of my changing my mind," the Duke replied. "I am only concerned with what is best for you."

"Then you know I cannot . . . leave him."

"Yes, I know," he said, "and I will stay with you."

She looked at him in a startled fashion.

"There is no need for you to do that. I shall be quite . . . safe."

"I would not like to risk it," he said. "By now everybody will know that your father is dead, and there are many things in this room that would interest the Collectors. Robbers who are prepared to rob the Tombs would not hesitate to rob you."

"I have our . . . servants . . . here," Irisa said.

"I feel that in an emergency I would be more protection than they could be," the Duke insisted. "What I would like to do, if you will allow me, is to send your servant to the yacht and tell them I shall not be returning. I will also order something for us to eat."

"I could . . . cook you . . . something," Irisa said a little vaguely.

"What I want you to do," the Duke answered fir

ly, "is to lie down. You are sensible enough to realise that
you have had a severe shock. When the meal is ready I
will let you know. In the meantime, rest. Try to believe,
as you said just now, that one day you and your father
will meet again."

As he said the words he thought that they were very
unlike anything he had ever thought or said before, and
certainly something he would never have believed if he
had not seen that strange vision in the sanctuary in Karnak.

But there was no time to think of that now.

Irisa went to her room, which was situated on the
other side of the Sitting-Room. Then the Duke called
the servant and, having scribbled his instructions on a
piece of paper, sent him off to the yacht.

Only when he had gone and the Duke started to
wander round the Sitting-Room, looking at the collec-
tion of Egyptian antiques which Irisa's father had accumulated, did he wonder what construction his party would
put on his absence.

He had made no explanation in the note he had
written to Harry. He had merely said that he would not
return as he was staying with a friend who needed him.
He had added a list of the food and drink he wanted.

As he could find no envelope on the table which was
obviously used as a desk, he merely folded the note,
handed it to the servant, and told him to hurry as quickly
as he could to the yacht on the other side of the river.

The Egyptian was obviously extremely impressed
that the Duke should be the owner of such a large and
magnificent craft.

He bowed low, his fingers touching his forehead,
and by the light of the stars now coming out the Duke
watched him running in his flat sandals over the sand.

Then as he looked round the room again to decide
where later he could make himself comfortable, he thought
this was an adventure that he had never foreseen and

could not possibly have imagined might happen on what was entirely a pleasure trip.

Yet he knew that this small room with its wooden walls, cheap furniture, and priceless relics from the past was also a part of the spell-binding mystery of Egypt which had enthralled and enchanted him ever since he had steamed through the lotus-shaped Delta into the Nile.

He had been propelled relentlessly towards Luxor, where fate, or perhaps one of the animal-headed gods, had decided that Irisa should be waiting for him in the Temple.

Chapter Six

The Duke spent a far more comfortable night than he had expected, because his valet Jenkins had arrived with the food and had brought what he would require for the night.

Jenkins was always invaluable in a crisis, and without asking any questions except to elicit that the Duke intended to stay in the Mission House, he procured, by some means of his own, a native bed.

It was only the usual structure of a frame on four legs with rope webbing as a support, but when there were blankets laid on it and a pillow it was easy for the Duke to sleep.

Before this he had sent Irisa's servant to the Hotel, and he had come back with the information that among the guests there was a retired Clergyman.

The Duke then wrote a note asking the Clergyman to perform the Burial Service the following morning.

He felt that it was the right thing in the circumstances, although he was aware that Irisa would have been quite content for her father to be buried in consecrated ground without a Service.

When he could think of nothing else for him to do, and the carpenter, having measured the dead man, had promised the coffin would be ready first thing in the morning, the Duke went to Irisa's bedroom to tell her that dinner was ready.

Jenkins had laid everything out on the table in the centre of the Sitting-Room, and he had also found several other candles in their carved wooden candle-sticks, which he had lit so that the room was lighter and without shadows.

When the Duke knocked on Irisa's door she opened it and he saw that she had changed her gown for another made in the same simple way.

He also thought she had been crying, but he could not be sure, since she was still calm and controlled.

"Come and have something to eat," he said, "and for the moment do not worry about anything else."

"I have been writing letters to the Missionary Society in England," she replied, "and also to the Anglican Bishop in Cairo, who asked Papa to take the Services here until the Church they are building is finished."

The Duke told her that there was a retired Clergyman staying at the Winter Palace, and she exclaimed:

"How kind of you to think of it! I thought Papa would have to be buried without any prayers but mine."

"And mine," the Duke said quietly.

She gave him a glance of gratitude, then sat down at the table on the chair that Jenkins pulled out for her.

"Thank you," she said to him. "I can see you have saved me a great deal of work, and I am most grateful."

"It's a pleasure, Miss," Jenkins answered, and went into the small kitchen to collect the first course.

The food the Duke had ordered was cold, but it was certainly delicious, and he was pleased to notice that Irisa ate quite a considerable amount and did not protest when Jenkins filled her glass with wine.

They talked very little while the valet was waiting on them, and only when he had cleared away the dishes and left the room did Irisa say:

"Please . . . do not trouble to stay . . . here tonight. I promise you I shall be quite . . . safe, and I do not . . . wish to take you from your . . . friends."

"My friends will amuse themselves without me," the Duke said, "and I am still concerned with your safety."

He spoke positively, and he liked the way she accepted that he was determined to do what he wished and ceased arguing with him.

Instead she said:

"You will understand that I want to stay . . . with Papa a little . . . longer before I go to . . . bed."

"Of course," the Duke agreed, "and I am quite prepared to sit reading until you are willing to try to sleep."

She thought he was telling her in a subtle way that it would be foolish to stay up all night and that with the ordeal of the Funeral ahead of her tomorrow she should rest.

She hesitated a moment. Then she said:

"I think perhaps it would interest you to read some of the notes Papa made about the Temples and Tombs since he came to Luxor."

"You mean he has written down his findings?"

"His findings and his thoughts, which I am sure one day will be proved true."

"Then there is nothing I would like more than to read them," the Duke said, "and I shall always, Irisa, regret deeply that I did not meet you father."

He smiled before he added:

"You will have to make up for my disappointment by telling me of the things which I want to know but was unable to ask him."

Irisa opened a drawer in the table which the Duke had thought was used as a desk and took out several manuscript-books from what he could see was a large pile of them.

"I think perhaps you will find it best to start with the last one and work backwards," she said. "As I told you, when we first came here Papa was sceptical about many things."

"I will read them in whichever order you tell me to," the Duke answered quietly.

As he spoke, Jenkins came from the kitchen. He had packed up the dishes in a basket and now he set it down on the floor.

"Is there anything else Your Grace requires?" he asked. "I've put Your Grace's razors in the washing-room and I'll be back first thing in the morning."

"Thank you," the Duke said, "and, Jenkins, I shall require two stewards to pack up all the ornaments in this room. It would be best if they could obtain wooden boxes so that nothing will be broken, and they will require plenty of newspaper with which to wrap each object."

Jenkins looked round.

"I'll see to it, Your Grace."

He picked up the basket and bowed to Irisa.

"Good-night, Miss! Good-night, Your Grace!"

When he had shut the door that led to the verandah, they heard his footsteps receding down the wooden steps.

"He is so kind," Irisa said, "but I am giving you all this . . . trouble."

"It is a repayment for what you have given me in the past," the Duke said, "and will, I hope, continue to do in the future."

He spoke lightly, wanting her to smile, and she said:

"I wish I had been able to tell Papa what happened today in the sanctuary. He would have been so interested and he would certainly have written it down."

"I have a feeling that his notes would be of inestimable value to a great number of people if they could read them," the Duke said, "and that means they must be published."

He felt for a moment that Irisa would refuse, thinking that what her father had written would be too personal. Then she said:

"If you could arrange that, it would justify everything Papa did in the life he chose against a great deal of opposition."

As she spoke she became very conscious that her father was separated from them only by a wooden door, and she added:

"I hope he . . . knows what you have . . . suggested."

Without another word she walked into the room where her father lay.

The Duke sat down in a wicker chair, thinking that nobody would believe it if he told them the strange things that had happened to him since he had come to Luxor.

He put the manuscript-books down on his knees and looked round the room. He was quite certain, as he had been when he first saw them, that many of the Egyptian carvings, statues, and bowls were very valuable.

"There are Collectors all over world," he said to himself, "who would wish to possess that small statue of the Pharaoh with the cobra-sign on his forehead."

There was another of a hawk-headed god which he was certain any Museum would covet.

He decided that before he allowed Irisa to sell even one of them he would not only have them all examined by the best Egyptologist in London, but he would also learn a great deal about such things himself, so as to make certain she was not cheated.

'I thought I was a knowledgeable man,' he thought with a sigh, 'and yet I have just discovered I am a complete ignoramous about a Kingdom which goes back to 3,200 B.C.'

It was two hours before the door of the bedroom opened and Irisa came out carrying the candle which had stood by the bed.

She closed the door quietly, and as the Duke rose to his feet, she did not speak to him but merely gave him a faint smile as she walked past him towards her own room.

He knew, because she did not talk, that she was transported by her prayers and her love of her father until she was with him in the world to which he had gone rather than in the earthly one he had left behind.

As the door of her bedroom closed, the Duke knew that she was aware that he would understand, just as he had known instinctively what she was feeling.

The notes he had been reading were so absorbing, so interesting, that he thought it was a pity to have to go to bed.

Then he knew that because of his long ride during the morning he was physically tired even though mentally he had never felt more alert.

He partially undressed, put on the long blue cotton robe which Jenkins had left ready for him, and lay down on the native bed, finding it surprisingly comfortable.

As he did so, he remembered that on his instructions Jenkins had brought with him a small revolver and placed it in the pocket of his gown.

He drew it out, put it down on a chair beside the bed which also held a candle, and then with a last look round at the treasures he was guarding as well as Irisa, he blew out the light.

*   *   *

He had been asleep for perhaps two hours when he awoke, conscious of danger.

He did not move but only listened, and was sure that something unusual had disturbed his sleep.

At first he could only hear the familiar sounds of the night, an owl hooting, a dog barking in the distance, and indistinct sounds to which it was impossible to put a name but which were doubtless the movements of rats or other small animals which would have gone unnoticed in the daytime.

He thought he heard a child crying, then much nearer, in fact he was certain it was outside on the verandah, there was a sound that could only have been made by a human being.

The door was locked, and after Jenkins had left them and Irisa had gone to her father's room the Duke had pushed home a heavy bolt.

He was sure that the sound he heard came from the window, and it flashed through his mind that that would be the easiest way for a thief to enter the house or even to put in his hand and try to grasp anything within reach.

He considered what he should do, and, sitting up in bed, he swung his feet onto the floor and reached first for his revolver, then for a box of matches.

He managed to hold both the revolver and the box in his left hand, then struck a match. It failed to light and he took out another.

As he did so, he was aware that whoever was outside the window was standing still, and he thought, although it might have been his imagination, that he could hear heavy breathing.

Then as the match flared into flame and he lit the candle, he heard somebody scurrying away down the wooden steps, but so quietly that he was certain the man was bare-footed.

The Duke rose and walked to the window to pull back the curtains. The stars and the moon gave a light by which he could be sure the small garden was empty, but it was impossible to see far beyond the shrubs.

'It is a good thing I was here!' he thought.

He knew that if he had not been, Irisa would certainly have been robbed of her father's treasures, and if she had attempted to interfere she might have been injured.

The Tomb-robbers were completely ruthless, and he had heard from visitors to Cairo how they had looted the treasures that had been excavated and had not hesitated to murder those who tried to prevent them from taking away their spoils.

The Duke thought that if he had been alone he might have followed the man, who perhaps had an accomplice waiting for him, but he knew that it was more important to keep Irisa safe than to risk leaving her unprotected.

He stood for some time at the window, knowing that anybody watching would be able to see him clearly with the light behind him.

Then, thinking it was unlikely that the robbers would return, he went back to bed.

*   *   *

In the morning, thanks to the Duke's organisation, everything went smoothly.

He had paid for the coffin, which he was certain was more expensive than what Irisa would have chosen. By the time she came from her bedroom, pale but composed, her father had been lifted from the bed and into it.

The embalmers had come back to make sure their work had not deteriorated overnight, and had brought with them flowers which the Duke thought should be both inside and outside the coffin.

He saw that Irisa was wearing a gown in which he had not seen her before, again very simple, and the pale blue-grey of a pigeon's breast.

It gave her an ethereal appearance and the bonnet which she carried in her hand had ribbons of the same colour.

Then as if the Duke had asked the question she said as he looked at her:

"I have no black, and Papa always said that if one believed in eternal life either as a Christian or an Egyptian, it was hypocritical to mourn those who had left us but were not dead."

The Duke thought that this was a very different sentiment from that expressed by Queen Victoria, who mourned so excessively that she was still wearing the deepest black for the Prince Consort, who had died twenty-six years ago, but he merely said:

"Everything you tell me about your father, and everything I read last night, makes me realise he was a very exceptional person."

Irisa's eyes lit up and she replied:

"I wish he had known that . . . somebody like you had . . . said that about . . . him."

She did not wait for the Duke to reply but went to the bedroom, and although he did not follow her he could see her through the open door standing looking down at the coffin.

After a few minutes he told the men who were waiting outside to come in, put on the lid, and screw it down.

When they carried the coffin out onto the verandah,

the small garden was already filled with people and others were arriving every moment.

The Duke knew they were the men and women whom Irisa's father had served not by trying to convert them to Christianity but by tending them in their illnesses.

He had healed their children of the eye-disease which affected so many Egyptians, and because he had lived amongst them they felt he was always there when they needed him.

Because they had loved him when he was alive, they were prepared to revere him now that he was dead.

By the time the bearers had lifted the coffin onto their shoulders and moved away with Irisa and the Duke following, there was a crowd of silent mourners following them all the way to the small Cemetery.

There were half-a-dozen graves of Christians who had died since Irisa and her father had come to Luxor, all marked with cheap little wooden crosses.

The retired Clergyman, wearing a white surplice, was standing by the open grave with a prayer-book in his hand, and as soon as the coffin was lowered he started the words of the Burial Service.

It was very short. At the same time, the Duke could not help thinking it was the sort of Funeral he would like for himself, with no pomp and circumstance, no mourners in black crepe, veils, black morning-coats, and top-hats.

Instead there was just Irisa, looking like someone who had stepped out of a fairy-story or perhaps down from the engravings on a Temple, and the natives with their children standing outside the small Cemetery but watching with reverence all that was taking place within.

As the Service finished, Irisa dropped a lotus-flower, which the Duke realised now came from the Sacred Lake at Karnak, onto the coffin.

Then as the grave-diggers covered it with sand, her

lips moved and the Duke knew she was saying good-bye to her father.

After they had both thanked the Clergyman, they walked back in silence to the house while the natives dispersed to their own mud huts.

The children, as if released from the constriction of being quiet, were chasing one another round the palm trees and their voices and laughter seemed to fill the air with joy.

When they entered the house, the Duke saw as he had expected that Jenkins had breakfast ready for them.

Irisa, however, went quickly into her bedroom and he wondered if she was too upset to join him, but again with a self-control that was exceptional she returned in about five minutes to sit down at the table and drink the coffee which Jenkins poured out for her.

Only then did she realise that a great number of the ornaments in the room had gone, and when she looked at the Duke as if for explanation he said:

"Jenkins tells me my stewards have already packed and taken two large boxes to the yacht, and are now procuring more, with which they will return in a very short while."

As he said this, Irisa rose from the table and walked to the shelves where the pottery was arranged. She lifted down three pots and several attractively decorated tiles which were propped against the wall behind them.

"These are fakes," she said, "and I think perhaps they should be separated from the others."

"Fakes?" the Duke exclaimed. "How do you know?"

He thought as he looked at them that they appeared to be very much the same as the others, and in fact they were indistinguishable from the ones Irisa had not moved.

"There are craftsmen working all the time," she explained, "to copy what is to be found in the Museums or a genuine article which has been stolen from a Tomb."

"How do you know which are fakes?" the Duke asked.

Irisa smiled at him for the first time that morning.

"*You* should be able to know by instinct," she replied. "But for ordinary people there are certain tests—quite simple ones—that can be made to determine whether the glazing is hundreds of years old or was put on yesterday!"

She saw that the Duke was interested and added:

"You always have to be on your guard against fakes, whatever you are offered, for the Egyptians are very, very clever at such deceptions."

"You mean they have inherited the craftsmanship of their ancestors?" the Duke replied. "I intend to buy quite a number of objects to take home with me before I leave Egypt, and I shall certainly need your help, Irisa."

"I am sure you will find plenty of connoisseurs in Cairo who will be only too willing to advise you."

"I prefer to trust you."

He thought, although he was not sure, that she was pleased.

He looked again at the genuine pottery on the shelf and saw that beside them there was a flat stone which seemed somehow out-of-place.

Irisa followed the direction of his eyes.

"That is Papa's consecrated stone."

The Duke looked puzzled.

"A travelling Priest," she explained, "cannot expect to find a Church everywhere he goes, but with that stone, any place where he puts it has the sanctity of a consecrated building."

"I have never heard of that before!" the Duke exclaimed.

When breakfast was over the stewards returned with the boxes which they required for the rest of the treasures, which were being carried by native porters.

The Duke said nothing, but he smiled as he thought

how quickly the English, whatever their station in life, reacted to being waited on when they were on foreign soil. In England there was no question but that the stewards would have carried the boxes themselves.

While they were carefully packing each object wrapped thickly in newspaper, Irisa went from the room to pack her clothes.

There could not have been many of them, for all she possessed filled only two small leather trunks, which to judge from their appearance had travelled many dusty miles and been somewhat roughly used.

She came into the Sitting-Room to collect her father's manuscript-books, and by that time all the ornaments had gone, including the fakes which the Duke had told the stewards to pack separately.

Then in a voice which sounded a little helpless she said:

"What shall I . . . do with Papa's . . . clothes?"

"I think you might leave them," he replied, "although I doubt very much whether they will still be here when his successor arrives."

She nodded her head in agreement, and he said:

"Does anything else belong to you? I suppose the furniture goes with the house."

"Our servants will be paid for keeping it safe."

"I will give them some money."

She looked at him a little shyly as she explained:

"Papa always . . . saw to those . . . things. I have never . . . worried about it . . . until now."

"Then leave it to me," the Duke said.

"N-no . . . please . . .." Irisa began, but he interrupted:

"We can talk about your financial situation later, but I think now it is best to take you away from here, otherwise you will feel upset."

"Papa hated people who made . . . scenes," Irisa said simply.

The Duke thought there were tears in her eyes as she said good-bye to the servants who he learnt had waited on them ever since they had arrived in Luxor.

One, who was a middle-aged man, obviously had a deep affection for Irisa, calling down on her the blessing of the gods, then as if he suddenly remembered he was a Christian, he added: "And the blessing of the Lord God and His Holy Spirit!"

When finally the stewards, Jenkins, and the luggage had all gone, the Duke and Irisa left too, but not by the shortest way used by the others, but through the waste-land which led to the Temple of Luxor.

The people in the mud huts waved to them and several small children ran up with flowers for Irisa. Then as they stepped through the tall columns they were alone and the atmosphere of the Temple seemed to envelop them as if they belonged there.

They did not speak but went slowly through the great Courtyards and past the red granite statues until they reached the place where they had first seen each other.

The view over the river towards the Valley of the Kings was dazzling in the sunshine, and Irisa stood looking at it for a long time, until the Duke said gently:

"There is no need for you to say good-bye. We shall come here again."

"You are . . . sure? I feel as if I am leaving everything I have ever known and stepping into a strange and frightening world of which I am completely ignorant."

"It is something you have done before," he said, thinking of how he had seen her in the sanctuary raised on a litter and being carried towards the Pharaoh's Palace.

"It is much the . . . same," she said, reading his thoughts, "only then I was saying . . . good-bye to . . . you, but now I have said . . . good-bye to . . . Papa."

"As you said yourself," he answered, "life flows on like the river—the river you are going to cross now. But we will come back."

She smiled at him as if he had suddenly swept away the mist in which she had been enveloped and now it was clear.

"It will . . . be an . . . adventure!" the Duke replied.

He put out his hand and she put her fingers in his.

She had taken off the gloves she had worn during the Funeral and now he felt her fingers tighten on his, not from fear but as if she sought his strength and it gave her courage.

They walked down the steps to where the Duke had ordered the dinghy to be waiting for them.

He helped her into it and as they sat side by side in the cushioned stern and the sailors dipped their oars, he said:

"You must not be nervous of meeting my guests. They are all very charming people and you will like them."

He felt it was right that he should reassure her, but even as he spoke he wondered what Lily's reaction would be to having another very lovely woman on board.

Irisa gave a little smile.

"I do not suppose," she said, "that they will be more frightening than the cannibals that Papa and I encountered in the Congo, or Mtesa, the King of Buganda, who celebrated any significant dream with a human sacrifice—Christians were the usual choice."

"But you survived."

"Only by the skin of our teeth!" Irisa answered, and the Duke laughed.

It was still comparatively early despite the fact that they had been busy for hours, and when they boarded the yacht there was only Harry seated under the awning and reading the newspapers which were out-of-date.

He rose to his feet as soon as the Duke and Irisa appeared, and exclaimed:

"I am delighted to see you, Dasher! I was rather afraid you have been lost in the desert or incarcerated in the Tomb of some long-dead Pharaoh and we would have to excavate the whole mountain to find you."

"But as you see, I am very much alive," the Duke replied.

He turned to Irisa.

"May I introduce my oldest friend, Harry Settingham—Miss Irisa Garron."

He saw as he spoke that Harry was staring at Irisa with both surprise and admiration in his eyes.

Then he was aware as Harry looked back at him that there was something he wanted to tell him.

"I expect you would like first to go to your cabin," he said to Irisa, "and take off your bonnet."

He did not wait for her answer but began to lead the way down the companionway which led to the cabins.

Then Jenkins appeared and he said:

"Will you show Miss Irisa to her cabin, Jenkins? I want to have a word with Mr. Settingham."

"Of course, Your Grace."

Leaving Jenkins to provide Irisa with everything she needed and doubtless to unpack for her as well, the Duke hurried back the way he had come to find Harry waiting for him.

Because they were so closely attuned to each other, the Duke said without preamble:

"What has happened?"

"A great deal!" Harry replied. "And I know you will be astonished, but I doubt if it will upset you very much."

"What do you mean?"

"Lily has left!"

"Left!" the Duke exclaimed.

This was certainly something he had not expected.

"With Charlie!"

The Duke stared at Harry incredulously.

"What are you saying?"

"That Lily was astute enough to realise she had lost you, and cut her losses somewhat dramatically."

"Did you say she has left with Charlie?"

Harry's lips twisted in a wry smile.

"Ostensibly he has left for England to see to some financial deal that makes it imperative for him to be in London in person."

"And what is the truth?"

"That he and Lily have gone first to Cairo, and then I think they intend to visit Paris."

"Good God! What has Amy to say about all this?"

"I have not dared to discuss it with her. I was leaving that to you."

"Thank you!" the Duke answered sarcastically. "But Charlie! I would not have believed it of him!"

"Shall I tell you exactly what happened?" Harry asked. "She saw you yesterday evening with that lovely creature you have just brought aboard."

"Where did she see me?"

"Coming down the steps of the Temple and getting into a boat."

The Duke looked puzzled, knowing it was some little distance from where the yacht was moored. Then Harry explained:

"Charlie, Lily, and I were standing here, and we were watching the birds through a pair of binoculars which he told us were the strongest ever made. They certainly had fantastic magnifying power."

He paused, but the Duke did not speak, so he continued:

"Charlie had been looking at the birds in the palm

trees when suddenly Lily gave an exclamation and took the binoculars from his hands. She could see you quite clearly as you walked down the steps and helped a young woman into a boat."

The Duke was still silent and Harry went on:

"I knew Lily had been annoyed all day that you had gone off riding without seeing her, and she dragged us back from the Winter Palace far earlier than we intended, simply because she hoped to catch you as soon as you returned."

The Duke said nothing, but he was thinking that Lily must have been already annoyed the day before, when he had not joined her in his private cabin and that night had omitted to make love to her as she must have expected.

But he was in fact not concerned with Lily's feelings so much as with his own overwhelming relief that he had no explanations to make about Irisa.

Nor was Lily here waiting to continue a love-affair which had, he knew, come abruptly to an end the moment he had arrived in Luxor.

It was not only Irisa who had ended his feelings for Lily but the fact that Lily belonged to a world which for the moment had no interest for him, and her beauty had lost its power even to evoke his admiration, let alone his desire.

He was aware that if she were still on the yacht he would have felt somewhat guilty at expressing the suddenness of the change in his feelings, which he could no more control than the river beneath them could stop flowing.

He knew that he was interested, intrigued, and fascinated by what he had found in Egypt, to the point where it was difficult to think of anything else or to understand how Lily had ever aroused him.

"When we learnt you were not returning last night," Harry was saying, "Lily accepted the inevitable and cut her losses."

"With Charlie," the Duke murmured.

"As you say, with Charlie," Harry repeated.

As if the Duke felt he must help in a mess for which he knew he was responsible, he said:

"I can hardly believe that what you are telling me is the truth, but I am extremely concerned about Amy."

"Charlie was attracted to Lily the moment he saw her."

"I had no idea."

"I know that," Harry said. "You had made it very obvious that she was yours and it was a question of 'Keep off!' But Lily appreciated that Charlie is a very, very rich man."

"I am disgusted by the whole thing!" the Duke exclaimed sharply. "I am going below to have a word with Amy."

As he did so, he knew he was not only disgusted but apprehensive as to what Amy would say or do.

He was extremely fond of her and he had always thought of Charlie as one of his best friends, but that this should happen, clearly through his fault, was very awkward and embarrassing.

He knocked on the door of Amy's cabin and when she told him to come in he found her sitting in a chair, writing letters.

"May I come in?" the Duke asked.

"Yes, of course, Dasher," Amy replied. "I am glad you are back. I was beginning to be worried about you."

"I am very worried indeed about what I have just learnt," the Duke said.

He crossed the cabin to sit down in a chair beside her, and after a moment she said:

"I know it must be embarrassing for you. At the same time, let me assure you that Charlie will come back to me."

"You are sure of that?"

"But of course!" Amy answered. "This has happened before, and when the first excitement of feeling young and showing off to a woman young enough to be his daughter is over, Charlie finds that there are two things which matter in his life more than anything else."

"What are those?" the Duke asked.

"His son and me!"

Amy gave a little sigh.

"I think Charlie loves Jack, who as you know will be leaving Eton next year, more than anybody else in the whole world. Although I am not and never have been as beautiful as somebody like Lily, I understand him and I also love him, because when he is not playing the part of the Gay Cavalier, he is only a little boy who needs mothering."

The Duke took Amy's hand in his and kissed it.

"You are wonderful!"

"Not really," Amy contradicted. "I want to scratch her eyes out, pull her hair, and scream! But that would do no good, so I am just going to try and amuse myself until Charlie returns."

"He has behaved abominably!" the Duke exclaimed angrily.

"Men are only human," Amy said, "and Lily is very, very beautiful, and I understand she has an appetite for emeralds."

The Duke repressed a laugh.

"That is what Harry said, but how do you know?"

"She has persuaded Charlie to go to Cairo, and if she does not find what she wants there, Paris will doubtless supply everything she needs, and that will include gowns from the redoubtable Mr. Worth."

"I am glad we have found her out," the Duke said. "She certainly took me in."

He realised that Amy was looking at him a little quizzically and with a somewhat twisted smile.

"To me she was always too good to be true," she said after a moment, "and I never did believe all that nonsense about being clairvoyant."

"Of course! It was all a fake," the Duke said.

As he spoke he could hear Irisa saying in her soft voice:

"Always beware of fakes."

If he had been more astute and used his intelligence and instinct, he thought now, he would have been aware from the very beginning that Lily was not what she seemed, and her claim to being "fey" had merely been an act which had unfortunately ensnared poor Charlie.

"A fake!" he murmured to himself, and knew that in contrast he had brought on board what was real and undisputably genuine.

When he left Amy, telling her again how much he admired her, he went back to Harry.

He had waited for him, and as the Duke flung himself down in a comfortable chair he said:

"I am not going to ask any questions. I just want to know what is happening, where we are going, and what you intend to do about Miss Garron."

"What do you expect me to do?" the Duke asked.

"Well—and I suppose it is a question—who is she?"

"She is the daughter of a Missionary."

He saw the astonishment in his friend's face and it amused him.

"Her father is dead," the Duke explained. "We buried him this morning, and she wishes to return to England. Is that what you want to know?"

"I never imagined that Missionaries had beautiful daughters. It is usually their wives who cut their way single-handedly through the jungle and rout hundreds of blood-thirsty Zulus!"

"You have been reading too many boys' adventure-stories!" the Duke remarked. "At the same time, Irisa did say that more frightening than meeting you were the cannibals her father and she encountered in the Congo."

"I find that easier to believe than Lily's prophecies of rising shares and gigantic profits!"

"Amy says," the Duke remarked, "that this is not the first time Charlie has gone off, but he always comes home."

"I know that," Harry replied. "Three years ago he went to the South of France for three months with Philip Goodwin's wife."

"Good Lord! I had no idea of that!" the Duke exclaimed.

"Everybody hushed it up for Amy's sake, and when he returned we pretended it had never happened."

"What happened to Philip's wife?"

"Consoled herself with a Greek ship-owner, I believe. Anyway, Philip refused to divorce her, so they are still married, although he has since involved himself with quite a few attractive creatures."

"I cannot think why you never tell me these things," the Duke complained.

"The answer to that is quite easy," Harry answered. "You are not interested."

The Duke was aware that that was true.

He was not interested in gossip and he did not care who ran away with whom, when he was living his own life to the full and concentrating on the things which he felt at that particular moment were important to him.

Now he had something much more interesting to concentrate on, but in an entirely different manner from anything he had known before.

He suddenly had an urge to be with Irisa, to talk to

her, to hear her soft voice telling him things which he found completely and utterly absorbing.

He thought perhaps she was staying down in her cabin because she had sensed that he wanted to talk to Harry alone.

Without explaining his reason for doing so, he got up and walked away to find her. Harry watched him go and for a moment his eyes were puzzled.

Then there was a smile on his lips, as if he had found the answer to a question.

He picked up the newspaper again.

* * *

Down below, the Duke found Jenkins coming from his own cabin.

"Where is Miss Irisa?" he asked.

In answer, Jenkins pointed to the cabin next to his, which had been occupied by Lily.

For a moment the Duke felt annoyed.

Then he told himself that it was the second-best cabin in the yacht and, as Lily was no longer using it, it had seemed obvious to Jenkins that he should install Irisa there.

Then as he thought about it, although it had not occurred to him before, it was exactly where he wanted her to be.

She was lovely, far more beautiful than Lily could ever be, and in a very different manner.

She was also, although until this moment he had been too bemused by all she had shown and told him to realise it, very desirable.

There was a light in the Duke's eyes, a light which had glowed over the years a great many times and which Harry would have recognised.

With a smile on his lips he knocked on the cabin door.

Chapter Seven

There was no answer, and when the Duke entered the cabin he found the reason for Irisa's silence. She was fast asleep.

She had lain down on top of the bed, having taken off only her bonnet and shoes, her cheek was turned against the pillow, and she was sleeping the sleep of complete exhaustion.

The Duke stood looking down at her.

Then he crossed the cabin and pulled the curtains over the port-holes before he went out, very quietly closing the door behind him.

He found Jenkins and said:

"Miss Irisa is asleep, Jenkins, and I think it would be wise to leave her."

"Of course, Your Grace," Jenkins agreed. "I thought as how she was very brave after her father died, but it always takes it out of one."

"Naturally," the Duke agreed. "See that she is not disturbed, and when she wakes, suggest that she stay in bed until dinner-time."

He went up on deck and found that James and Amy had joined Harry and were sipping from long glasses which continued fresh fruit-juice.

"There you are, Dasher!" James exclaimed. "I was beginning to think you had been eaten by the crocodiles!"

"Not yet," the Duke replied, "and that reminds me—I want to swim this afternoon, but farther up the river. I do not like to be too near to human habitation."

"What has happened to Miss Garron?" Harry asked.

"She is asleep," the Duke replied.

He sat down beside Amy, who said:

"Harry has been telling me that her father was buried this morning. How tragic for her, and she does not sound very much like a Missionary."

"I cannot believe you have often met one," the Duke replied, and Amy laughed.

"No, that is true, but I always think they must be outstandingly brave to go out into the wilds, protected only by their faith."

"I have heard that Africa has accounted for the lives of many Missionaries," James remarked, "and I agree with Amy, even if such people are misguided, they are certainly brave."

They had luncheon, and a short time afterwards the Duke was rowed up the river to find himself a place where he could bathe in what he was sure was clean water, and without too many interested observers.

He swam against the stream, feeling he was using every muscle in his body and that it was as good an exercise as riding one of his own horses round the Race-Course, or sparring with Harry, which they often did in his private Gymnasium at the Castle.

The Duke tried not to think of the wonders that were to be found on the banks of the Nile.

He felt it would somehow be unfair to explore them without Irisa, and if he thought about them when she was not there, there would be too many questions in his mind which needed answers.

Feeling pleasantly relaxed after his swim, he was rowed back to the yacht to find that his guests had left a message to say that they had gone to the Winter Palace Hotel, where Amy wished to see some friends who had just arrived from England.

The Duke had no intention of joining them.

Instead he went to his own private cabin and started to read the manuscripts that Irisa had given him, written by her father. He found them absorbing and they explained many things he wanted to know.

Then, because he too had spent a somewhat restless night, he dozed in his armchair, to awake with a start when Jenkins came to tell him that it was time to change for dinner.

"Is Miss Irisa awake?" the Duke enquired.

"Yes, Your Grace. She woke at about four o'clock and I took her some tea and persuaded her to settle down for a few hours longer. Now she's taking a bath, and I'm sure looking forward to joining Your Grace for dinner."

The Duke thought Jenkins sounded like an efficient Nanny, and he thought that any man, whatever his position in life, would feel protective towards Irisa.

He himself certainly did, and as he bathed and dressed he wondered what sort of life she would find waiting for her when she reached England.

It seemed strange that she had not visited the country of her origin since she was a baby. Yet he supposed that having travelled so much and encountered people of such varied kinds, she would somehow be able to take it in her stride.

He found that this supposition was correct when she met his friends.

Thinking she might be shy of meeting them alone, when he was dressed the Duke sent Jenkins to ask if she was ready, and he returned to say that she was.

As the Duke came from his cabin and saw that the door of Irisa's was open, he walked in to see her arranging her hair in front of the mirror.

She turned to smile at him, and he thought that now that she had rested and the lines of suffering were no longer dark beneath her eyes, she looked very beautiful and very spring-like.

"I am ashamed at my indolence!" she exclaimed as the Duke appeared. "Your valet tells me you have been swimming, and I am envious."

"You can swim?" the Duke asked in surprise.

"Like a fish!" Irisa replied. "I assure you if I had not been able to I would have been drowned a dozen times when Papa and I had to cross swollen rivers, and once in a monsoon we were caught in a rising flood which drowned quite a number of native children before we could rescue them."

"I shall insist not only that your father's book must be published but that you should write one yourself."

Irisa laughed.

"Do you really believe that anybody would be interested in the perils of being a Missionary?"

"I would be interested," the Duke answered, and she smiled at him again.

Only as she rose from the stool on which she was sitting did he realise that she was not wearing evening-dress but again one of the simple gowns that he suspected she had made herself.

It was an attractively patterned muslin such as could be bought cheaply in any native Bazaar, but on Irisa it seemed as right as if she were clothed in cloth of gold, and it was difficult to think that anything could be more becoming.

The Duke did not say anything, but with a lack of self-consciousness that he realised was exceptional she said to Amy as soon as they had been introduced:

"I hope you will forgive me for not possessing anything more elaborate in the way of evening-gowns, but Papa and I were never invited out to dinner except with Bedouin Chieftains when they roasted a whole sheep."

"You look charming!" Amy said.

The Duke, seeing the expression in James's eyes, and in Harry's, realised they thought the same.

As diner progressed, he was aware that Irisa was quiet but attentive, still appearing to be supremely un-self-conscious that she was doing anything unusual, and he knew too that Harry approved of her.

The Duke was too close to his oldest friend not to be aware that he had disliked Lily and obviously mistrusted her.

But it was quite clear that his feelings where Irisa was concerned were very different, and the Duke found it rather surprising.

He knew that Harry, like some of his other friends, was always afraid that he would be exploited because he was so rich and of such social importance.

Since Harry knew nothing of his mental affinity with Irisa, he thought that it might be expected that he would suspect her of being a penniless Missionary's daughter intent on making use of him and getting herself invited on his yacht after such a short acquaintance.

But there was not that mocking, sarcastic note in his voice that Harry had used towards Lily, and when after dinner Amy had the chance of speaking to the Duke alone, she said:

"That child is delightful! Do you think she would resent it if I offered to lend her anything she might need while we are on the yacht together?"

"I am sure she would be delighted," the Duke answered.

As they were five, there was no question of their playing cards, so they sat on deck listening to the sound of voices and laughter coming from the other side of the river.

All the time the Duke was vividly conscious of the moonlight on the Temple of Luxor, and he felt as if the mystery of it was vibrating towards him.

Then as if Amy found it difficult to keep up a brave front, and she too felt emotionally exhausted after what had happened earlier in the day, she rose to her feet.

"I am going to bed," she said. "I do not want to break up the party, but I am tired."

"I think I . . . too should go . . . to bed," Irisa said.

She glanced at the Duke as she spoke, as if for his approval, and he answered:

"I think it is a good idea, and I am sure that tomorrow there will be some interesting but quite tiring things for us to do."

"Then come along, Irisa," Amy said. "You and I will leave the men to gossip, we hope about us, but it is more likely to be about horses!"

"Good-night, Your Grace!" Irisa said.

She gave him a little curtsey which was very graceful.

* * *

About an hour later the Duke went to his own cabin, where Jenkins was waiting for him.

"It's been very hot today, Your Grace," he said as he helped him out of his tight-fitting evening-coat.

"Yes, and I enjoyed my swim. I have an idea I am losing weight."

"I wouldn't be surprised," Jenkins said gloomily, "and that means Your Grace's clothes'll all have to be altered when we gets back to London."

"There is plenty of time to worry about that," the Duke replied.

He put on one of his thin cotton robes like the one he had worn last night, which in the heat were far more comfortable than silk.

When his valet had left him, he went to the port-hole to look out at the stars.

It was then that he was vividly conscious that he was looking at them alone, and that Irisa was in the next cabin.

As he thought of her, he felt her beauty and her desirability sweep over him and arouse in him emotions that he recognised because they were so familiar.

"She is lovely!" the Duke told himself. "Lovelier than any other woman I have ever seen!"

He did not stop to think or even to consider whether it was right or wrong. He only knew that he wanted to be with Irisa, and he had never denied himself anything he wanted.

Closing the port-hole, he walked across the cabin and a second later was standing outside her door.

He wondered for a moment whether he should knock, then thought if she was already asleep it would be unkind to wake her.

He turned the handle, then he saw that she was sitting up in bed with one of her father's manuscript-books in her hands.

As he looked at her he realised for the first time that he was seeing her with her hair down, and it was something which subconsciously he had longed to see.

It flowed over her shoulders with just a faint wave in

it and made her look like the classical pictures of a nymph
or a mermaid.

She was wearing a very simple nightgown of white
muslin that was fastened at the neck and had little frills
over her wrists.

But the light beside her bed revealed the curves of
her breasts and the Duke was aware that she was very
human and a woman.

It flashed through his mind that she might be surprised
at his appearance, or perhaps shocked, but when she saw
him she smiled and exclaimed:

"I am so glad you have come to say good-night to
me. I have something very exciting to tell you."

It was not the reception the Duke had expected,
but he walked to the bed and sat down on it, facing her.

"I thought you would like to know that I have
remembered what your name was when you were a . . .
soldier and I was the . . . bride of a . . . Pharaoh."

"I am prepared to believe anything you tell me,"
the Duke answered.

Looking at her, he thought that nobody could be
more alluring, more exciting, and because his whole body
was throbbing he found it hard to concentrate on what
she was saying.

"Your name was Alexi," she said. "Does that seem
significant?"

"No, I do not think so."

"It is Greek."

"Yes, of course," he agreed, "and now that I think of
it, Iris is also a Greek name. Do you suppose we might
have come to Egypt from Greece?"

"It is certainly possible."

"Then we must go there," the Duke said, "and perhaps we shall see what happened before you arrived
here."

Irisa clasped her hands together.

"That would be too . . . wonderful to . . . contemplate, but . . . perhaps . . ."

She hesitated.

"Perhaps?" the Duke prompted.

". . . you want to go somewhere else with your friends. They were very kind to me tonight, and I think for the first time I realised that in this life you and I live in very different worlds."

"I suppose that is true," the Duke said slowly.

He was thinking of his life in England, his Castle, his horses, of the parties at Marlborough House, of the piles of invitation-cards that arrived every day for him wherever he was.

Then his thoughts came back to Irisa.

She looked like a lotus-bud, but she was alone, and he knew, as surely as if she had said so, that for the moment the future for her was an empty, barren desert stretching away interminably to an indefinite horizon.

Irisa was watching his face and he knew she was reading his thoughts.

"I have no . . . wish," she said softly, "to be an . . . encumbrance, and perhaps I should . . . return to England without . . . troubling you."

The words were spoken quite simply and he knew that she was thinking not of herself but of him.

For a moment there was silence. Then he said:

"Will you marry me, Irisa?"

She looked at him as if she did not understand what he had said.

Then there was a light in her eyes that seemed as dazzling as the sun on the water of the Sacred Lake.

The Duke waited, somehow unable to say any more, conscious only of the radiance in Irisa's eyes as she asked almost inaudibly:

"Is . . . that what you . . . want?"

"I have only just realised, Irisa," he replied, "that I

want it more than I have ever wanted anything in my whole life. After all, it would be a fitting end to our story."

"Not an . . . end," Irisa whispered, "but . . . a beginning."

Slowly, as if he was moving forward in time, the Duke took both her hands in his and raised them one after the other to his lips.

Then as his mouth felt the softness of her skin, the spell which had made him feel that it was hard to speak and almost impossible to move broke. He put his arms round her, his lips sought hers, and he kissed her.

As he did so he realised that it was very different from any kiss he had ever given or received before. There was none of the fiery passion that he usually associated with desire.

It was something very different, very wonderful, ecstatic and spiritual.

He wanted Irisa not only with his body but with his mind and his soul. At the same time, he approached her with a reverence, as if she were sacred in a way he had never felt about any other woman.

Her lips were very soft, yielding, and innocent, and as he knew he was the first man who had kissed her in this life, he was tender and gentle.

Then when he felt her respond to his need of her, his kisses became more possessive and more demanding.

They were both breathless when he raised his head to say:

"How can this have happened? I know now that you are what I have been looking for and missing all my life, and it was an instinct stronger than thought which brought me all the way to Egypt to find you."

"I love . . . you! Oh, Alexi, I love . . . you as I . . . always . . . have!"

"For how long?"

"From the . . . beginning of . . . time . . . perhaps even . . . before . . . that."

The Duke made a sound of happiness and triumph.

Then he was kissing her again, kissing her until she felt overwhelmed and put up her hands with a little murmur of protest.

Instantly she was free.

"Forgive me, my darling," he said. "I worship you, and at the same time I am reassuring myself that you are human and will not vanish onto one of the columns and another thousand years will pass before I find you again."

"Wherever I . . . am, I shall . . . always love . . . you."

"Is it true, really true, that you loved me before we met?" the Duke asked.

"I have always been aware of you in my dreams. The first time Papa took me to the sanctuary at Karnak, I saw, as we both saw it yesterday . . . my arrival in . . . Egypt."

"Alexi!" the Duke said softly. "So that was my name!"

"You do not mind my calling you that?"

"No, of course not," he answered. "In fact, it is very appropriate that I should have a new name, because, thanks to you, I have been reborn. In the future, 'The Dasher,' as he is known in England, will cease to exist."

Irisa gave a little cry.

"No, I would not have you . . . changed! You have . . . become what you are over . . . thousands of years . . . in perhaps thousands of lives . . . and through your good deeds you have . . . gained the position you have now."

"And you?"

She gave a little sigh.

"Perhaps I behaved badly or forgot to do good, which is why I have come back as I have."

"I am content for you to be just as you are," the Duke said.

Then he was kissing her again.

It was a long while later when he sensed that while

the radiance was still shining in her eyes like the stars that shone in the sky outside, she was tired, and he said:

"I am going to leave you now, my lovely one. Go to sleep and think only that I love you and you are to be my wife."

"I wish I could tell Papa about . . . us," Irisa whispered.

"I am sure he knows," the Duke answered.

He thought it was the most unexpected thing for him to say, and yet he knew it was true.

He kissed her again very gently and tenderly, and when she had cuddled herself down in the bed he pulled the sheet up to her chin.

"Good-night, my precious," he said very softly. "Dream of me."

"It would be . . . difficult for me . . . not to."

He looked down at her for a long moment before he turned out the light.

Then as he went from the cabin he felt as if his whole world had turned upside down and he could hardly believe that his feelings were not just a figment of his imagination.

One thing was irrefutably true—he had found the love that was different and for which, although he had denied it, he had always been seeking.

*   *   *

The stars were shining in the great arc of the Heavens and a crescent moon was moving slowly up the sky.

The yacht was anchored for the night and everything was still and quiet.

The Duke put his arm round Irisa as they stood on deck, looking out into the star-strewn darkness, knowing that tomorrow they would be seeing the Temples of Abu Simbel.

As the same time, they were finding for the moment that nothing could be more wonderful and exciting than their discovery of each other, and every day it seemed to the Duke they grew closer.

In fact, their happiness increased until he felt as if it vibrated from them like the light which shone from the stars.

To Irisa it was as if she had stepped into a Paradise that she could hardly believe was not just a vision in the darkness and had no substance in reality.

Yet, every time the Duke touched her, she knew it was very real, and although they had loved each other in many others lives, in this they were man and woman, and it was too wonderful to express in words.

"Are you happy, my darling?" the Duke asked.

"So happy," she answered, "that all I want to say is: 'I love you! I love you!' over and over again until you are tired of hearing it."

"I shall never be that," he replied, "and I keep thanking the gods that they sent me anybody so perfect as you."

Irisa thought that the gods had certainly blessed them as she had known they would when they had been married the morning after the Duke had come to her cabin and asked her to be his wife.

She had slept without dreaming, and even while unconscious she had a feeling of happiness that was with her when she awoke to find Jenkins pulling back the curtains over the port-holes.

"It's eight o'clock, Miss!" he said. "His Grace asks for you to be ready for him in an hour's time!"

"But of course!" Irisa exclaimed. "How can I have slept so late? I usually rise at six."

"It's the best thing you could do, Miss," Jenkins said firmly. "I've brought you a small breakfast, but there's plenty more if you're hungry."

Irisa looked at the tray he had put down beside her
and exclaimed:

"It is more than enough. Thank you!"

Jenkins went towards the door, and as he did so he
said:

"I'll have your bath ready for you, Miss, when you're
finished, and His Lordship asks if you'll wear the blue
gown. He says you'll know the one he means."

Irisa smiled.

She knew it was the gown she was wearing when
they had first met. Although it was not one of her newest
and the Duke had been right in thinking she had made it
herself, she knew that that particular dress would always
have a special significance for them.

She enjoyed the cool, scented bath that Jenkins had
prepared for her, and she was just ready when he came
into her cabin carrying something on a tray.

"I was just going to ask if His Grace wishes to go
ashore," Irisa said, "in which case I must wear my bonnet."

"His Grace asks if you'll wear this, Miss," Jenkins
said, holding out the tray.

Irisa looked in surprise at what it contained. She
saw it was a wreath of lotus-buds, just pink tinged, and
skilfully woven together with a few small green leaves.

For a moment she did not understand. Then suddenly
she did, and to Jenkins, watching her, her face seemed
transfigured.

She placed the wreath on her head, then as she
went a little shyly up the companionway and onto the
deck, she found the Duke waiting for her with a bouquet
of lotus-flowers.

He handed it to her and there was no need for
words.

She only looked into his grey eyes and knew that

she loved him overwhelmingly and that he loved her.

They were rowed across the river to the steps which led into the Temple of Luxor, and as the Duke drew her without speaking through the passage of the columns, she knew where they were going.

When they reached the place where they had first met, she saw first a profusion of brilliant flowers which lay at the foot of the pillars, and then the same Clergyman who had buried her father waiting for them in his white surplice.

Behind him on a plinth which acted as an altar was the consecrated stone which had belonged to her father.

The Service was short, and yet as they were made man and wife Irisa felt that the gods were all round them and were giving them their blessings.

Only when they were alone and walking back down the steps to where the boat was waiting did Irisa say a little incoherently:

"How could you have . . . thought of . . . anything so wonderful . . . so perfect as for us to be married in the Temple where we . . . found each . . . other?"

"I could not imagine anywhere more appropriate," the Duke replied, "and, my sweet, as we took our vows, I felt as if it were the gods themselves who gave you to me."

She looked at him with her soul in her eyes because it was what she had been thinking herself.

"Only . . . you would understand," she said.

When they had gone back to the yacht, the Duke took her down to his private cabin to put his arms round her.

"You are mine! My wife!" he said. "Whatever happened in the past, we are now together, and I swear that as long as we shall live, I will never lose you."

Then he was kissing her until Irisa felt that they had

found a special Heaven in which there was nobody else, not even the gods but only themselves.

* * *

A long time later, when the Duke had sent for champagne with which they could drink their own health, Irisa realised that the yacht was moving.

She had been so bemused by the wonder of the Duke's kisses that she had not realised the engines were throbbing beneath them.

Now she asked,

"Where are we going?"

"On our honeymoon," the Duke replied, "and alone."

She looked at him questioningly, and he explained:

"My friends have tactfully agreed to stay at the Winter Palace Hotel as my guests until we return. Then we will take them as far as Cairo or Alexandria, from where they will make their own way home."

"Do they . . . mind?" Irisa asked.

"No, because they want us to be happy," the Duke replied. "They sent you their good wishes, my darling. But I would not let them see you, because I want you to myself."

"That . . . is what I want too," Irisa said, "but how can you have arranged everything so . . . cleverly and so . . . perfectly?"

"I think you have inspired me to think in a different way from what I have ever done in the past," the Duke answered, "and all I wish to do is to imagine how I can make you happy."

"I am happy, so very . . . very happy!" Irisa cried.

She suddenly put out her hand to touch the Duke.

"You are quite certain you are not just a part of my vision, and in a moment you will vanish?"

"Later I will make you believe I am very real." the Duke said in his deep voice.

For a moment they could only look into each other's eyes. Then Irisa gave a little sigh.

"I am so glad I do not have to go to England . . . alone . . . I was . . . frightened of meeting my . . . grandfather."

"Is he so ferocious?"

"He was to Papa when he became a Missionary! He cut him off with the proverbial shilling."

"Why should he think it so wrong?"

"Because he wanted Papa, who had always wanted to be a Doctor, to take Holy Orders so that he could take over one of the many livings my grandfather has on his Estate."

The Duke looked surprised because it sounded as if Irisa's grandfather was a land-owner. Then suddenly he exclaimed:

"Garron! I thought it sounded familiar! Are you a relative of Lord Tregarron?"

"He is my grandfather!"

"I had no idea. Why did you not tell me?"

"There was no reason to do so," Irisa replied, "and Papa was so hurt by his father's refusal to have anything to do with him that we never spoke of his family."

"I have met Lord Tregarron at Race-Meetings. Now that I think of it, I have always thought him a proud, unbending man."

"I am sure he is, and he expected his sons to obey him. Papa's elder brother went into the family Regiment, as he was told to do, but Papa wanted to see the world, to travel and explore! When his father insisted he should become a country Vicar, he ran away."

"To become a Missionary."

"He saw a lot of the world, if rather uncomfortably. It . . . killed Mama, but Papa was . . . happy after he came to . . . Luxor."

"It was fate," the Duke said, "that I should find you here."

He was perfectly content to marry Irisa even if she was a nobody, but he knew that the fact that she was the granddaughter of Lord Tregarron would make it easy for her to enter the Social World to which sometime he would have to return.

But there was no hurry for the moment. There would be many places for them to see and explore together, the first being Greece.

"I adore you," he said. "And all I can think of is you."

* * *

The reality of being in the Duke's arms and learning about love was so rapturous and divine that Irisa was sure they were held in the magic spell in which the Egyptians had always believed.

There was the magic of the Temples, the barren hills, the sunshine, the Nile itself, and now with her head on the Duke's shoulder as she looked at the reflection of the moon and stars on the water, she said:

"This river has meant so much in our lives. It carried me to the Pharaoh, and it took you away from me. Not it has brought you to me again and we are together! And it will flow on, even when we are no longer here."

"It is the river of love," the Duke answered. "And remember, my precious, that love, like life, cannot die."

Irisa smiled.

"Now you are teaching me."

"That is what I want to do where love is concerned," the Duke said, "and because I love you so wildly and passionately, I am at this moment, my adorable one, a man and not a god, and I want you to be closer to me than you are at the moment."

As he spoke he bent and kissed not her lips, as she expected, but the softness of her neck where a little pulse was beating frantically because he excited her.

"I love ... you ... oh ... Alexi," she whispered. "I love ... you."

"I will worship you," he answered, "from now until the stars fall from the sky and the world ceases to exist."

Then with the smoothness of the river flowing beneath them he drew her from the deck.

He knew that in the secrecy of their cabin they would find a love that was older than the earth, but still young and creative with every new life—the love which is eternity.

ABOUT THE AUTHOR

BARBARA CARTLAND, the world's most famous romantic novelist, who is also an historian, playwright, lecturer, political speaker and television personality, has now written over 300 books.

She has also had many historical works published and has written four autobiographies as well as the biographies of her mother and that of her brother Ronald Cartland, who was the first Member of Parliament to be killed in W.W. II. This book has a preface by Sir Winston Churchill and has just been republished with an introduction by Sir Arthur Bryant.

Barbara Cartland has sold 200 million books over the world, more than half of these in the U.S.A. She broke the world record in 1975 by writing twenty-three books and the four subsequent years with 20, 21, 23 and 24. In addition her album of love songs has just been published, sung with the Royal Philharmonic Orchestra.

Barbara Cartland, who is a Dame of the Order of St. John of Jerusalem has championed the cause for old people and founded the first Romany Gypsy Camp in the world.

Barbara Cartland is deeply interested in Vitamin Therapy and is President of the British National Association for Health. Her book the *Magic of Honey* has sold in millions all over the world.

She has a magazine *The World of Romance* and her Barbara Cartland Romantic World Tours will, in conjunction with British Airways, carry travelers to England, Egypt, India, France, Germany and Turkey.

Barbara Cartland

The world's bestselling author of romantic fiction. Her stories are always captivating tales of intrigue, adventure and love.

☐	13830	THE DAWN OF LOVE	$1.75
☐	14504	THE KISS OF LIFE	$1.75
☐	14503	THE LIONESS AND THE LILY	$1.75
☐	13942	LUCIFER AND THE ANGEL	$1.75
☐	14084	OLA AND THE SEA WOLF	$1.75
☐	14133	THE PRUDE AND THE PRODIGAL	$1.75
☐	13032	PRIDE AND THE POOR PRINCESS	$1.75
☐	13984	LOVE FOR SALE	$1.75
☐	14248	THE GODDESS AND THE GAIETY GIRL	$1.75
☐	14360	SIGNPOST TO LOVE	$1.75
☐	14361	FROM HELL TO HEAVEN	$1.75
☐	14585	LOVE IN THE MOON	$1.95
☐	13985	LOST LAUGHTER	$1.75
☐	14509	AFRAID	$1.75
☐	14902	WINGED MAGIC	$1.95
☐	14922	A PORTRAIT OF LOVE	$1.95

Buy them at your local bookstore or use this handy coupon: